The Princess Priscilla's Fortnight

by

Elizabeth von Arnim

I

Her Grand Ducal Highness the Princess Priscilla of Lothen-Kunitz was up
to the age of twenty-one a most promising young lady. She was not only
poetic in appearance beyond the habit of princesses but she was also of
graceful and appropriate behaviour. She did what she was told; or, more
valuable, she did what was expected of her without being told. Her father,
in his youth and middle age a fiery man, now an irritable old gentleman
who liked good food and insisted on strictest etiquette, was proud of her on
those occasions when she happened to cross his mind. Her mother, by birth
an English princess of an originality uncomfortable and unexpected in a
royal lady that continued to the end of her life to crop up at disconcerting
moments, died when Priscilla was sixteen. Her sisters, one older and one
younger than herself, were both far less pleasing to look upon than she was,
and much more difficult to manage; yet each married a suitable prince and
each became a credit to her House, while as for Priscilla,--well, as for
Priscilla, I propose to describe her dreadful conduct.

But first her appearance. She was well above the average height of woman;
a desirable thing in a princess, who, before everything, must impress the
public with her dignity. She had a long pointed chin, and a sweet mouth
with full lips that looked most kind. Her nose was not quite straight, one

side of it being the least bit different from the other,--a slight crookedness that gave her face a charm absolutely beyond the reach of those whose features are what is known as chiselled. Her skin was of that fairness that freckles readily in hot summers or on winter days when the sun shines brightly on the snow, a delicate soft skin that is seen sometimes with golden eyelashes and eyebrows, and hair that is more red than gold. Priscilla had these eyelashes and eyebrows and this hair, and she had besides beautiful grey-blue eyes--calm pools of thought, the court poet called them, when her having a birthday compelled him to official raptures; and because everybody felt sure they were not really anything of the kind the poet's utterance was received with acclamations. Indeed, a princess who should possess such pools would be most undesirable--in Lothen-Kunitz nothing short of a calamity; for had they not had one already? It was what had been the matter with the deceased Grand Duchess; she would think, and no one could stop her, and her life in consequence was a burden to herself and to everybody else at her court. Priscilla, however, was very silent. She had never expressed an opinion, and the inference was that she had no opinion to express. She had not criticized, she had not argued, she had been tractable, obedient, meek. Yet her sisters, who had often criticized and argued, and who had rarely been obedient and never meek, became as I have said the wives of appropriate princes, while Priscilla,--well, he who runs may read what it was that Priscilla became.

But first as to where she lived. The Grand Duchy of Lothen-Kunitz lies in the south of Europe; that smiling region of fruitful plains, forest-clothed hills, and broad rivers. It is one of the first places Spring stops at on her way up from Italy; and Autumn, coming down from the north sunburnt, fruit-laden, and blest, goes slowly when she reaches it, lingering there with her serenity and ripeness, her calm skies and her windless days long after the Saxons and Prussians have lit their stoves and got out their furs. There figs can be eaten off the trees in one's garden, and vineyards glow on the hillsides. There the people are Catholics, and the Protestant pastor casts no shadow of a black gown across life. There as you walk along the white roads, you pass the image of the dead Christ by the wayside; mute reminder to those who would otherwise forget of the beauty of pitifulness and love. And there, so near is Kunitz to the soul of things, you may any morning get into the train after breakfast and in the afternoon find yourself drinking coffee in the cool colonnades of the Piazza San Marco at Venice.

Kunitz is the capital of the duchy, and the palace is built on a hill. It is one of those piled-up buildings of many windows and turrets and battlements on which the tourist gazes from below as at the realization of a childhood's dream. A branch of the river Loth winds round the base of the hill, separating the ducal family from the red-roofed town along its other bank. Kunitz stretches right round the hill, lying clasped about its castle like a necklet of ancient stones. At the foot of the castle walls the ducal orchards and kitchen gardens begin, continuing down to the water's edge and clothing the base of the hill in a garment of blossom and fruit. No fairer sight is to be seen than the glimpse of these grey walls and turrets rising out of a cloud of blossom to be had by him who shall stand in the market place of Kunitz and look eastward up the narrow street on a May morning; and if he who gazes is a dreamer he could easily imagine that where the setting of life is so lovely its days must of necessity be each like a jewel, of perfect brightness and beauty.

The Princess Priscilla, however, knew better. To her unfortunately the life within the walls seemed of a quite blatant vulgarity; pervaded by lacqueys, by officials of every kind and degree, by too much food, too many clothes, by waste, by a feverish frittering away of time, by a hideous want of privacy, by a dreariness unutterable. To her it was a perpetual behaving according to the ideas officials had formed as to the conduct to be expected of princesses, a perpetual pretending not to see that the service offered was sheerest lip-service, a perpetual shutting of the eyes to hypocrisy and grasping selfishness. Conceive, you tourist full of illusions standing free down there in the market place, the frightfulness of never being alone a moment from the time you get out of bed to the time you get into it again. Conceive the deadly patience needed to stand passive and be talked to, amused, taken care of, all day long for years. Conceive the intolerableness, if you are at all sensitive, of being watched by eyes so sharp and prying, so eager to note the least change of expression and to use the conclusions drawn for personal ends that nothing, absolutely nothing, escapes them. Priscilla's sisters took all these things as a matter of course, did not care in the least how keenly they were watched and talked over, never wanted to be alone, liked being fussed over by their ladies-in-waiting. They, happy girls, had thick skins. But Priscilla was a dreamer of dreams, a poet who never wrote poems, but whose soul though inarticulate was none the less saturated with the desires and loves from which poems are born. She, like her sisters, had actually known no other states; but then she dreamed of them continuously, she desired them continuously, she read of them continuously; and though there was only one person who knew she did these things I suppose one person is enough in the way of encouragement if your mind is bent on rebellion. This old person, cause of all the mischief that followed, for without his help I do not see what Priscilla could have done, was the ducal librarian--*Hofbibliothekar*, head, and practically master of the wonderful collection of books and manuscripts whose mere catalogue made learned mouths in distant parts of Europe water and learned lungs sigh in hopeless envy. He too had officials under him, but they were unlike the others: meek youths, studious and short-sighted, whose business as far as Priscilla could see was to bow themselves out silently whenever she and her lady-in-waiting came in. The librarian's name was Fritzing; plain Herr Fritzing originally, but gradually by various stages at last arrived at the dignity and sonorousness of Herr Geheimarchivrath Fritzing. The Grand Duke indeed had proposed to ennoble him after he had successfully taught Priscilla English grammar, but Fritzing, whose spirit dwelt among the Greeks, could not be brought to see any desirability in such a step. Priscilla called him Fritzi when her lady-in-waiting dozed; dearest Fritzi sometimes even, in the heat of protest or persuasion. But afterwards, leaving the room as solemnly as she had come in, followed by her wide-awake attendant, she would nod a formally gracious "Good afternoon, Herr Geheimrath," for all the world as though she had been talking that way the whole time. The Countess (her lady-in-waiting was the Countess Irmgard von Disthal, an ample slow lady, the unmarried daughter of a noble house, about fifty at this time, and luckily--or unluckily--for Priscilla, a great lover of much food and its resultant deep slumbers) would bow in her turn in as stately a manner as her bulk permitted, and with a frigidity so pronounced that in any one less skilled in shades of deportment it would have resembled with a singular completeness a sniff of scorn. Her frigidity was perfectly justified. Was she not a *hochgeboren*, a member of an ancient house, of luminous pedigree as far back as one could possibly see? And was he not the son of an obscure Westphalian farmer, a person who in his youth had sat barefoot watching pigs? It is true he had learning, and culture, and a big head with plenty of brains in it, and the Countess Disthal had a small head, hardly any brains, no soul to speak of, and no education. This, I say, is true; but it is also neither here nor there. The Countess was the Countess, and Fritzing was a nobody, and the condescension she showed him was far more grand ducal than anything in that way that Priscilla could or ever did produce.

Fritzing, unusually gifted, and enterprising from the first--which explains the gulf between pig-watching and *Hofbibliothekar*--had spent ten years in Paris and twenty in England in various capacities, but always climbing higher in the world of intellect, and had come during this climbing to speak English quite as well as most Englishmen, if in a statelier, Johnsonian manner. At fifty he began his career in Kunitz, and being a lover of children took over the English education of the three princesses; and now that they had long since learned all they cared to know, and in Priscilla's case all of grammar at least that he had to teach, he invented a talent for drawing in Priscilla, who could not draw a straight line, much less a curved one, so that she should still be able to come to the library as often as she chose on the pretext of taking a drawing-lesson. The Grand Duke's idea about his daughters was that they should know a little of everything and nothing too well; and if Priscilla had said she wanted to study Shakespeare with the librarian he would have angrily forbidden it. Had she not had ten years for studying Shakespeare? To go on longer than that would mean that she was eager, and the Grand Duke loathed an eager woman.

But he had nothing to say against a little drawing; and it was during the drawing-lessons of the summer Priscilla was twenty-one that the Countess Disthal slept so peacefully. The summer was hot, and the vast room cool and quiet. The time was three o'clock--immediately, that is, after luncheon. Through the narrow open windows sweet airs and scents came in from the bright world outside. Sometimes a bee would wander up from the fruit-gardens below, and lazily drone round shady corners. Sometimes a flock of pigeons rose swiftly in front of the windows, with a flash of shining wings. Every quarter of an hour the cathedral clock down in the town sent up its slow chime. Voices of people boating on the river floated up too, softened to melodiousness. Down at the foot of the hill the red roofs of the town glistened in the sun. Beyond them lay the sweltering cornfields. Beyond them forests and villages. Beyond them a blue line of hills. Beyond them, said Priscilla to herself, freedom. She sat in her white dress at a table in one of the deep windows, her head on its long slender neck, where the little rings of red-gold hair curled so prettily, bent over the drawing-board, her voice murmuring ceaselessly, for time was short and she had a great many things to say. At her side sat Fritzing, listening and answering. Far away in the coolest, shadiest corner of the room slumbered the Countess. She was lulled by the murmured talk as sweetly as by the drone of the bee.

"Your Grand Ducal Highness receives many criticisms and much advice on the subject of drawing from the Herr Geheimrath?" she said one day, after a lesson during which she had been drowsily aware of much talk.

"The Herr Geheimrath is most conscientious," said Priscilla in the stately, it-has-nothing-to-do-with-you sort of tone she found most effectual with the Countess; but she added a request under her breath that the *lieber Gott* might forgive her, for she knew she had told a fib.

Indeed, the last thing that Fritzing was at this convulsed period of his life was what his master would have called conscientious. Was he not encouraging the strangest, wickedest, wildest ideas in the Princess? Strange and wicked and wild that is from the grand ducal point of view, for to Priscilla they seemed all sweetness and light. Fritzing had a perfect horror of the Grand Duke. He was everything that Fritzing, lean man of learning, most detested. The pleasantest fashion of describing the Grand Duke will be simply to say that he was in all things, both of mind and body, the exact opposite of Fritzing. Fritzing was a man who spent his time ignoring his body and digging away at his mind. You know the bony aspect of such men. Hardly ever is there much flesh on them; and though they are often ugly enough, their spirit blazes at you out of wonderful eyes. I call him old Fritzing, for he was sixty. To me he seemed old; to Priscilla at twenty he seemed coeval with pyramids and kindred hoarinesses; while to all those persons who were sixty-one he did not seem old at all. Only two things could have kept this restless soul chained to the service of the Grand Duke, and those two things were the unique library and Priscilla. For the rest, his life at Kunitz revolted him. He loathed the etiquette and the fuss and the intrigues of the castle. He loathed each separate lady-in-waiting, and every one of the male officials. He loathed the vulgar abundance and inordinate length and frequency of the meals, when down in the town he knew there were people a-hungered. He loathed the lacqueys with a quite peculiar loathing, scowling at them from under angry eyebrows as he passed from his apartment to the library; yet such is the power of an independent and scornful spirit that though they had heard all about Westphalia and the pig-days never once had they, who made insolence their study, dared be rude to him.

Priscilla wanted to run away. This, I believe, is considered an awful thing to do even if you are only a housemaid or somebody's wife. If it were not considered awful, placed by the world high up on its list of Utter Unforgivablenesses, there is, I suppose, not a woman who would not at some time or other have run. She might come back, but she would surely have gone. So bad is it held to be that even a housemaid who runs is unfailingly pursued by maledictions more or less definite according to the education of those she has run from; and a wife who runs is pursued by social ruin, it being taken for granted that she did not run alone. I know at least two wives who did run alone. Far from wanting yet another burden added to them by adding to their lives yet another man, they were anxiously endeavouring to get as far as might be from the man they had got already. The world, foul hag with the downcast eyes and lascivious lips, could not believe it possible, and was quick to draw its dark mantle of disgrace over their shrinking heads. One of them, unable to bear this, asked her husband's pardon. She was a weak spirit, and now lives prostrate days, crushed beneath the unchanging horror of a husband's free forgiveness. The other took a cottage and laughed at the world. Was she not happy at last, and happy in the right way? I go to see her sometimes, and we eat the cabbages she has grown herself. Strange how the disillusioned find their peace in cabbages.

Priscilla, then, wanted to run away. What is awful in a housemaid and in anybody's wife became in her case stupendous. The spirit that could resolve it, decide to do it without being dragged to it by such things as love or passion, calmly looking the risks and losses in the face, and daring everything to free itself, was, it must be conceded, at least worthy of respect. Fritzing thought it worthy of adoration; the divinest spirit that had ever burned within a woman. He did not say so. On the contrary, he was frightened, and tried angrily, passionately, to dissuade. Yet he knew that if she wavered he would never forgive her; she would drop at once from her high estate into those depths in his opinion where the dull average of both sexes sprawled for ever in indiscriminate heaps. Priscilla never dreamed of wavering. She, most poetic of princesses, made apparently of ivory and amber, outwardly so cool and serene and gentle, was inwardly on fire. The fire, I should add, burnt with a very white flame. Nothing in the shape of a young man had ever had the stoking of it. It was that whitest of flames that leaps highest at the thought of abstractions--freedom, beauty of life, simplicity, and the rest. This, I would remark, is a most rare light to find burning in a woman's breast. What she was, however, Fritzing had made her. True the material had been extraordinarily good, and for ten years he had done as he liked with it. Beginning with the simpler poems of Wordsworth--he detested them, but they were better than soiling her soul with Longfellow and Mrs. Hemans--those lessons in English literature, meant by the authorities to be as innocuous to her as to her sisters, had opened her eyes in a way nothing else could have done to the width of the world and the littleness of Kunitz. With that good teacher, as eager to lead as she to follow, she wandered down the splendid walks of culture, met there the best people of all ages, communed with mighty souls, heard how they talked, saw how they lived, and none, not one, lived and talked as they lived and talked at Kunitz.

Imagine a girl influenced for ten years, ten of her softest most wax-like years, by a Fritzing, taught to love freedom, to see the beauty of plain things, of quietness, of the things appertaining to the spirit, taught to see how ignoble it is, how intensely, hopelessly vulgar to spend on one's own bodily comforts more than is exactly necessary, taught to see a vision of happiness possible only to those who look to their minds for their joys and not to their bodies, imagine how such a girl, hearing these things every afternoon almost of her life, would be likely to regard the palace mornings and evenings, the ceremonies and publicity, all those hours spent as though she were a celebrated picture, forced everlastingly to stand in an attitude considered appropriate and smile while she was being looked at.

"No one," she said one day to Fritzing, "who hasn't himself been a princess can have the least idea of what it is like."

"Ma'am, it would be more correct to say herself in place of himself."

"Well, they can't," said Priscilla.

"Ma'am, to begin a sentence with the singular and continue it with the plural is an infraction of all known rules."

"But the sentiments, Fritzi--what do you think of the sentiments?"

"Alas, ma'am, they too are an infraction of rules."

"What is not in this place, I should like to know?" sighed Priscilla, her chin on her hand, her eyes on that distant line of hills beyond which, she told herself, lay freedom.

She had long ago left off saying it only to herself. I think she must have been about eighteen when she took to saying it aloud to Fritzing. At first, before he realized to what extent she was sick for freedom, he had painted in glowing colours the delights that lay on the other side of the hills, or for that matter on this side of them if you were alone and not a princess. Especially had he dwelt on the glories of life in England, glories attainable indeed only by the obscure such as he himself had been, and for ever impossible to those whom Fate obliges to travel in state carriages and special trains. Then he had come to scent danger and had grown wary; trying to put her off with generalities, such as the inability of human beings to fly from their own selves, and irrelevancies such as the amount of poverty and wretchedness to be observed in the east of London; refusing to discuss France, which she was always getting to as the first step towards England, except in as far as it was a rebellious country that didn't like kings; pointing out with no little temper that she had already seen England; and finishing by inquiring very snappily when her Grand Ducal Highness intended to go on with her drawing.

Now what Priscilla had seen of England had been the insides of Buckingham Palace and Windsor Castle; of all insides surely the most august. To and from these she had been conveyed in closed carriages and royal trains, and there was so close a family likeness between them and Kunitz that to her extreme discomfort she had felt herself completely at home. Even the presence of the Countess Disthal had not been wanting. She therefore regarded this as not seeing England at all, and said so. Fritzing remarked tartly that it was a way of seeing it most English people would envy her; and she was so unable to believe him that she said Nonsense.

But lately her desires had taken definite shape so rapidly that he had come to dread the very word hill and turn cold at the name of England. He was being torn in different directions; for he was, you see, still trying to do what other people had decided was his duty, and till a man gives up doing that he will certainly be torn. How great would be the temptation to pause here and consider the mangled state of such a man, the wounds and weakness he will suffer from, and how his soul will have to limp through life, if it were not that I must get on with Priscilla.

One day, after many weeks of edging nearer to it, of going all round it yet never quite touching it, she took a deep breath and told him she had determined to run away. She added an order that he was to help her. With her most grand ducal air she merely informed, ordered, and forbade. What she forbade, of course, was the betrayal of her plans. "You may choose," she said, "between the Grand Duke and myself. If you tell him, I have done with you for ever."

Of course he chose Priscilla.

His agonies now were very great. Those last lacerations of conscience were terrific. Then, after nights spent striding, a sudden calm fell upon him. At length he could feel what he had always seen, that there could not be two duties for a man, that no man can serve two masters, that a man's one clear duty is to be in the possession of his soul and live the life it approves: in other and shorter words, instead of leading Priscilla, Priscilla was now leading him.

She did more than lead him; she drove him. The soul he had so carefully tended and helped to grow was now grown stronger than his own; for there was added to its natural strength the tremendous daring of absolute inexperience. What can be more inexperienced than a carefully guarded young princess? Priscilla's ignorance of the outside world was pathetic. He groaned over her plans--for it was she who planned and he who listened-- and yet he loved them. She was a divine woman, he said to himself; the sweetest and noblest, he was certain, that the world would ever see.

Her plans were these:

First, that having had twenty-one years of life at the top of the social ladder she was now going to get down and spend the next twenty-one at the bottom of it. (Here she gave her reasons, and I will not stop to describe Fritzing's writhings as his own past teachings grinned at him through every word she said.)

Secondly, that the only way to get to the bottom being to run away from Kunitz, she was going to run.

Thirdly, that the best and nicest place for living at the bottom would be England. (Here she explained her conviction that beautiful things grow quite naturally round the bottom of ladders that cannot easily reach the top; flowers of self-sacrifice and love, of temperance, charity, godliness-- delicate things, with roots that find their nourishment in common soil. You could not, said Priscilla, expect soil at the top of ladders, could you? And as she felt that she too had roots full of potentialities, she must take them down to where their natural sustenance lay waiting.)

Fourthly, they were to live somewhere in the country in England, in the humblest way.

Fifthly, she was to be his daughter.

"Daughter?" cried Fritzing, bounding in his chair. "Your Grand Ducal Highness forgets I have friends in England, every one of whom is aware that I never had a wife."

"Niece, then," said Priscilla.

He gazed at her in silence, trying to imagine her his niece. He had two sisters, and they had stopped exactly at the point they were at when they helped him, barefoot, to watch Westphalian pigs. I do not mean that they had not ultimately left the little farm, gone into stockings, and married. It is their minds I am thinking of, and these had never budged. They were like their father, a doomed dullard; while Fritzing's mother, whom he resembled, had been a rather extraordinary woman in a rough and barbarous way. He found himself wholly unable to imagine either of his sisters the mother of this exquisite young lady.

These, then, baldly, were Priscilla's plans. The carrying of them out was left, she informed him, altogether to Fritzing. After having spent several anxious days, she told him, considering whether she ought to dye her hair black in order to escape recognition, or stay her own colour but disguise herself as a man and buy a golden beard, she had decided that these were questions Fritzing would settle better than she could. "I'd dye my hair at once," she said, "but what about my wretched eyelashes? Can one dye eyelashes?"

Fritzing thought not, and anyhow was decidedly of opinion that her eyelashes should not be tampered with; I think I have said that they were very lovely. He also entirely discouraged the idea of dressing as a man. "Your Grand Ducal Highness would only look like an extremely conspicuous boy," he assured her.

"I could wear a beard," said Priscilla.

But Fritzing was absolutely opposed to the beard.

As for the money part, she never thought of it. Money was a thing she never did think about. It also, then, was to be Fritzing's business. Possibly things might have gone on much longer as they were, with a great deal of planning and talking, and no doing, if an exceedingly desirable prince had not signified his intention of marrying Priscilla. This had been done before by quite a number of princes. They had, that is, not signified, but implored. On their knees would they have implored if their knees could have helped them. They were however all poor, and Priscilla and her sisters were rich; and how foolish, said the Grand Duke, to marry poor men unless you are poor yourself. The Grand Duke, therefore, took these young men aside and crushed them, while Priscilla, indifferent, went on with her drawing. But now came this one who was so eminently desirable that he had no need to do more than merely signify. There had been much trouble and a great deal of delay in finding him a wife, for he had insisted on having a princess who should be both pretty and not his cousin. Europe did not seem to contain such a thing. Everybody was his cousin, except two or three young women whom he was rude enough to call ugly. The Kunitz princesses had been considered in their turn and set aside, for they too were cousins; and it seemed as if one of the most splendid thrones in Europe would either have to go queen-less or be sat upon by somebody plain, when fate brought the Prince to a great public ceremony in Kunitz, and he saw Priscilla and fell so violently in love with her that if she had been fifty times his cousin he would still have married her.

That same evening he signified his intention to the delighted Grand Duke, who immediately fell to an irrelevant praising of God.

"Bosh," said the Prince, in the nearest equivalent his mother-tongue provided.

This was very bad. Not, I mean, that the Prince should have said Bosh, for he was so great that there was not a Grand Duke in Europe to whom he might not have said it if he wanted to; but that Priscilla should have been in imminent danger of marriage. Among Fritzing's many preachings there had been one, often repeated in the strongest possible language, that of all existing contemptibilities the very most contemptible was for a woman to marry any one she did not love; and the peroration, also extremely forcible, had been an announcement that the prince did not exist who was fit to tie her shoestrings. This Priscilla took to be an exaggeration, for she had no very great notion of her shoestrings; but she did agree with the rest. The subject however was an indifferent one, her father never yet having asked her to marry anybody; and so long as he did not do so she need not, she thought, waste time thinking about it. Now the peril was upon her, suddenly, most unexpectedly, very menacingly. She knew there was no hope from the moment she saw her father's face quite distorted by delight. He took her hand and kissed it. To him she was already a queen. As usual she gave him the impression of behaving exactly as he could have wished. She certainly said very little, for she had long ago learned the art of being silent; but her very silences were somehow exquisite, and the Grand Duke thought her perfect. She gave him to understand almost without words that it was a great surprise, an immense honour, a huge compliment, but so sudden that she would be grateful to both himself and the Prince if nothing more need be said about it for a week or two--nothing, at least, till formal negotiations had been opened. "I saw him yesterday for the first time," she pleaded, "so naturally I am rather overwhelmed."

Privately she had thought, his eyes, which he had never taken off her, kind and pleasant; and if she had known of his having said Bosh who knows but that he might have had a chance? As it was, the moment she was alone she sent flying for Fritzing. "What," she said, "do you say to my marrying this man?"

"If you do, ma'am," said Fritzing, and his face seemed one blaze of white conviction, "you will undoubtedly be eternally lost."

II

They fled on bicycles in the dusk. The goddess Good Luck, who seems to have a predilection for sinners, helped them in a hundred ways. Without her they would certainly not have got far, for both were very ignorant of the art of running away. Once flight was decided on Fritzing planned elaborately and feverishly, got things thought out and arranged as well as he, poor harassed man, possibly could. But what in this law-bound world can sinners do without the help of Luck? She, amused and smiling dame, walked into the castle and smote the Countess Disthal with influenza, crushing her down helpless into her bed, and holding her there for days by the throat. While one hand was doing this, with the other she gaily swept the Grand Duke into East Prussia, a terrific distance, whither, all unaware of how he was being trifled with, he thought he was being swept by an irresistible desire to go, before the business of Priscilla's public betrothal should begin, and shoot the roebucks of a friend.

The Countess was thrust into her bed at noon of a Monday in October. At three the Grand Duke started for East Prussia, incognito in a motor--you know the difficulty news has in reaching persons in motors. At four one of Priscilla's maids, an obscure damsel who had been at the mercy of the others and was chosen because she hated them, tripped out of the castle with shining eyes and pockets heavy with bribes, and caused herself to be whisked away by the afternoon express to Cologne. At six, just as the castle guard was being relieved, two persons led their bicycles through the archway and down across the bridge. It was dark, and nobody recognized them. Fritzing was got up sportingly, almost waggishly--heaven knows his soul was not feeling waggish--as differently as possible from his usual sober clothes. Somehow he reminded Priscilla of a circus, and she found it extremely hard not to laugh. On his head he had a cap with ear-pieces that hid his grey hair; round his neck a gaudy handkerchief muffled well about his face; immense goggles cloaked the familiar overhanging eyebrows and deep-set eyes, goggles curiously at variance with the dapper briskness of his gaitered legs. The Princess was in ordinary blue serge, short and rather shabby, it having been subjected for hours daily during the past week to rough treatment by the maid now travelling to Cologne. As for her face and hair, they were completely hidden in the swathings of a motor-veil.

The sentinels stared rather as these two figures pushed their bicycles through the gates, and undoubtedly did for some time afterwards wonder who they could have been. The same thing happened down below on the bridge; but once over that and in the town all they had to do was to ride straight ahead. They were going to bicycle fifteen miles to Rühl, a small town with a railway station on the main line between Kunitz and Cologne. Express trains do not stop at Rühl, but there was a slow train at eight which would get them to Gerstein, the capital of the next duchy, by midnight. Here they would change into the Cologne express; here they would join the bribed maid; here luggage had been sent by Fritzing,--a neat bag for himself, and a neat box for his niece. The neat box was filled with neat garments suggested to him by the young lady in the shop in Gerstein where he had been two days before to buy them. She told him of many other articles which, she said, no lady's wardrobe could be considered complete without; and the distracted man, fearing the whole shop would presently be put into trunks and sent to the station to meet them, had ended by flinging down two notes for a hundred marks each and bidding her keep strictly within that limit. The young lady became very scornful. She told him that she had never heard of any one being clothed from head to foot inside and out, even to brushes, soap, and an umbrella, for two hundred marks. Fritzing, in dread of conspicuous masses of luggage, yet staggered by the girl's conviction, pulled out a third hundred mark note, but added words in his extremity of so strong and final a nature, that she, quailing, did keep within this limit, and the box was packed. Thus Priscilla's outfit cost almost exactly fifteen pounds. It will readily be imagined that it was neat.

Painfully the two fugitives rode through the cobbled streets of Kunitz. Priscilla was very shaky on a bicycle, and so was Fritzing. Some years before this, when it had been the fashion, she had bicycled every day in the grand ducal park on the other side of the town. Then, tired of it, she had given it up; and now for the last week or two, ever since Fritzing had told her that if they fled it would have to be on bicycles, she had pretended a renewed passion for it, riding every day round and round a circle of which the chilled and astonished Countess Disthal, whose duty it was to stand and watch, had been the disgusted central point. But the cobbles of Kunitz are very different from those smooth places in the park. All who bicycle round Kunitz know them as trying to the most skilful. Naturally, then, the fugitives advanced very slowly, Fritzing's heart in his mouth each time they passed a brightly-lit shop or a person who looked at them. Conceive how nearly this poor heart must have jumped right out of his mouth, leaving him dead, when a policeman who had been watching them strode suddenly into the middle of the street, put up his hand, and said, "Halt."

Fritzing, unstrung man, received a shock so awful that he obeyed by falling off. Priscilla, wholly unused to being told to halt and absorbed by the difficulties of the way, did not grasp that the order was meant for her and rode painfully on. Seeing this, the policeman very gallantly removed her from her bicycle by putting his arms round her and lifting her off. He set her quite gently on her feet, and was altogether a charming policeman, as unlike those grim and ghastly eyes of the law that glare up and down the streets of, say, Berlin, as it is possible to imagine.

But Priscilla was perfectly molten with rage, insulted as she had never been in her life. "How dare you--how dare you," she stammered, suffocating; and forgetting everything but an overwhelming desire to box the giant's ears she had actually raised her hand to do it, which would of course have been the ruin of her plan and the end of my tale, when Fritzing, recovering his presence of mind, cried out in tones of unmistakable agony, "Niece, be calm."

She calmed at once to a calm of frozen horror.

"Now, sir," said Fritzing, assuming an air of brisk bravery and guiltlessness, "what can we do for you?"

"Light your lamps," said the policeman, laconically.

They did; or rather Fritzing did, while Priscilla stood passive.

"I too have a niece," said the policeman, watching Fritzing at work; "but I light no lamps for her. One should not wait on one's niece. One's niece should wait on one."

Fritzing did not answer. He finished lighting the lamps, and then held Priscilla's bicycle and started her.

"I never did that for my niece," said the policeman.

"Confound your niece, sir," was on the tip of Fritzing's tongue; but he gulped it down, and remarking instead as pleasantly as he could that being an uncle did not necessarily prevent your being a gentleman, picked up his bicycle and followed Priscilla.

The policeman shook his head as they disappeared round the corner. "One does not light lamps for one's niece," he repeated to himself. "It's against nature. Consequently, though the peppery Fräulein may well be somebody's niece she is not his."

"Oh," murmured Priscilla, after they had ridden some way without speaking, "I'm deteriorating already. For the first time in my life I've wanted to box people's ears."

"The provocation was great, ma'am," said Fritzing, himself shattered by the spectacle of his Princess being lifted about by a policeman.

"Do you think--" Priscilla hesitated, and looked at him. Her bicycle immediately hesitated too, and swerving across the road taught her it would have nothing looked at except its handles. "Do you think," she went on, after she had got herself straight again, "that the way I'm going to live now will make me want to do it often?"

"Heaven forbid, ma'am. You are now going to live a most noble life--the only fitting life for the thoughtful and the earnest. It will be, once you are settled, far more sheltered from contact with that which stirs ignoble impulses than anything your Grand Ducal Highness has hitherto known."

"If you mean policemen by things that stir ignoble impulses," said Priscilla, "I was sheltered enough from them before. Why, I never spoke to one. Much less"--she shuddered--"much less ever touched one."

"Ma'am, you do not repent?"

"Heavens, no," said Priscilla, pressing onward.

Outside Rühl, about a hundred yards before its houses begin, there is a pond by the wayside. Into this, after waiting a moment peering up and down the dark road to see whether anybody was looking, Fritzing hurled the bicycles. He knew the pond was deep, for he had studied it the day he bought Priscilla's outfit; and the two bicycles one after the other were hurled remorsely into the middle of it, disappearing each in its turn with a tremendous splash and gurgle. Then they walked on quickly towards the railway station, infinitely relieved to be on their own feet again, and between them, all unsuspected, walked the radiant One with the smiling eyes, she who was half-minded to see this game through, giving the players just so many frights as would keep her amused, the fickle, laughing goddess Good Luck.

They caught the train neatly at Rühl. They only had to wait about the station for ten minutes before it came in. Hardly any one was there, and nobody took the least notice of them. Fritzing, after a careful look round to see if it contained people he knew, put the Princess into a second-class carriage labelled *Frauen*, and then respectfully withdrew to another part of the train. He had decided that second-class was safest. People in that country nearly always travel second-class, especially women,--at all times in such matters more economical than men; and a woman by herself in a first-class carriage would have been an object of surmise and curiosity at every station. Therefore Priscilla was put into the carriage labelled *Frauen*, and found herself for the first time in her life alone with what she had hitherto only heard alluded to vaguely as the public.

She sat down in a corner with an odd feeling of surprise at being included in the category *Frauen*, and giving a swift timid glance through her veil at the public confronting her was relieved to find it consisted only of a comfortable mother and her child.

I know not why the adjective comfortable should so invariably be descriptive of mothers in Germany. In England and France though you may be a mother, you yet, I believe, may be so without being comfortable. In Germany, somehow, you can't. Perhaps it is the climate; perhaps it is the food; perhaps it is simply want of soul, or that your soul does not burn with a fire sufficiently consuming. Anyhow it is so. This mother had all the good-nature that goes with amplitude. Being engaged in feeding her child with *belegte Brödchen*--that immensely satisfying form of sandwich--she at once offered Priscilla one.

"No thank you," said Priscilla, shrinking into her corner.

"Do take one, Fräulein," said the mother, persuasively.

"No thank you," said Priscilla, shrinking.

"On a journey it passes the time. Even if one is not hungry, thank God one can always eat. Do take one."

"No thank you," said Priscilla.

"Why does she wear that black thing over her face?" inquired the child. "Is she a witch?"

"Silence, silence, little worthless one," cried the mother, delightedly stroking his face with half a *Brödchen*. "You see he is clever, Fräulein. He resembles his dear father as one egg does another."

"Does he?" said Priscilla, immediately conceiving a prejudice against the father.

"Why don't she take that black thing off?" said the child.

"Hush, hush, small impudence. The Fräulein will take it off in a minute. The Fräulein has only just got in."

"Mutti, is she a witch? Mutti, Mutti, is she a witch, Mutti?"

The child, his eyes fixed anxiously on Priscilla's swathed head, began to whimper.

"That child should be in bed," said Priscilla, with a severity born of her anxiety lest, to calm him, humanity should force her to put up her veil. "Persons who are as intelligent as that should never be in trains at night. Their brains cannot bear it. Would he not be happier if he lay down and went to sleep?"

"Yes, yes; that is what I have been telling him ever since we left Kunitz"-- Priscilla shivered--"but he will not go. Dost thou hear what the Fräulein says, Hans-Joachim?"

"Why don't she take that black thing off?" whimpered the child.

But how could the poor Princess, however anxious to be kind, take off her veil and show her well-known face to this probable inhabitant of Kunitz?

"Do take it off, Fräulein," begged the mother, seeing she made no preparations to do so. "When he gets ideas into his head there is never peace till he has what he wants. He does remind me so much of his father."

"Did you ever," said Priscilla, temporizing, "try him with a little--just a little slap? Only a little one," she added hastily, for the mother looked at her oddly, "only as a sort of counter-irritant. And it needn't be really hard, you know--"

"*Ach*, she's a witch--Mutti, she's a witch!" shrieked the child, flinging his face, butter and all, at these portentous words, into his mother's lap.

"There, there, poor tiny one," soothed the mother, with an indignant side-glance at Priscilla. "Poor tiny man, no one shall slap thee. The Fräulein does not allude to thee, little son. The Fräulein is thinking of bad children such as the sons of Schultz and thy cousin Meyer. Fräulein, if you do not remove your veil I fear he will have convulsions."

"Oh," said the unhappy Priscilla, getting as far into her corner as she could, "I'm so sorry--but I--but I really can't."

"She's a witch, Mutti!" roared the child, "I tell it to thee again--therefore is she so black, and must not show her face!"

"Hush, hush, shut thy little eyes," soothed the mother, putting her hand over them. To Priscilla she said, with an obvious dawning of distrust, "But Fräulein, what reason can you have for hiding yourself?"

"Hiding myself?" echoed Priscilla, now very unhappy indeed, "I'm not hiding myself. I've got--I've got--I'm afraid I've got a--an affection of the skin. That's why I wear a veil."

"*Ach*, poor Fräulein," said the mother, brightening at once into lively interest. "Hans-Joachim, sleep," she added sharply to her son, who tried to raise his head to interrupt with fresh doubts a conversation grown thrilling. "That is indeed a misfortune. It is a rash?"

"Oh, it's dreadful," said Priscilla, faintly.

"*Ach*, poor Fräulein. When one is married, rashes no longer matter. One's husband has to love one in spite of rashes. But for a Fräulein every spot is of importance. There is a young lady of my acquaintance whose life-happiness was shipwrecked only by spots. She came out in them at the wrong moment."

"Did she?" murmured Priscilla.

"You are going to a doctor?"

"Yes--that is, no--I've been."

"Ah, you have been to Kunitz to Dr. Kraus?"

"Y--es. I've been there."

"What does he say?"

"That I must always wear a veil."

"Because it looks so bad?"

"I suppose so."

There was a silence. Priscilla lay back in her corner exhausted, and shut her eyes. The mother stared fixedly at her, one hand mechanically stroking Hans-Joachim, the other holding him down.

"When I was a girl," said the mother, so suddenly that Priscilla started, "I had a good deal of trouble with my skin. Therefore my experience on the subject is great. Show me your face, Fräulein--I might be able to tell you what to do to cure it."

"Oh, on no account--on no account whatever," cried Priscilla, sitting up very straight and speaking with extraordinary emphasis. "I couldn't think of it--I really positively couldn't."

"But my dear Fräulein, why mind a woman seeing it?"

"But what do you want to see it for?"

"I wish to help you."

"I don't want to be helped. I'll show it to nobody--to nobody at all. It's much too--too dreadful."

"Well, well, do not be agitated. Girls, I know, are vain. If any one can help you it will be Dr. Kraus. He is an excellent physician, is he not?"

"Yes," said Priscilla, dropping back into her corner.

"The Grand Duke is a great admirer of his. He is going to ennoble him."

"Really?"

"They say--no doubt it is gossip, but still, you know, he is a very handsome man--that the Countess von Disthal will marry him."

"Gracious!" cried Priscilla, startled, "what, whether he wants to or not?"

"No doubt he will want to. It would be a brilliant match for him."

"But she's at least a hundred. Why, she looks like his mother. And he is a person of no birth at all."

"Birth? He is of course not noble yet, but his family is excellent. And since it is not possible to have as many ailments as she has and still be alive, some at least must be feigned. Why, then, should she feign if it is not in order to see the doctor? They were saying in Kunitz that she sent for him this very day."

"Yes, she did. But she's really ill this time. I'm afraid the poor thing caught cold watching--dear me, only see how sweetly your little boy sleeps. You should make Levallier paint him in that position."

"Ah, he looks truly lovely, does he not. Exactly thus does his dear father look when asleep. Sometimes I cannot sleep myself for joy over the splendid picture. What is the matter with the Countess Disthal? Did Dr. Kraus tell you?"

"No, no. I--I heard something--a rumour."

"Ah, something feigned again, no doubt. Well, it will be a great match for him. You know she is lady-in-waiting to the Princess Priscilla, the one who is so popular and has such red hair? The Countess has an easy life. The other two Princesses have given their ladies a world of trouble, but Priscilla--oh, she is a model. Kunitz is indeed proud of her. They say in all things she is exactly what a Princess should be, and may be trusted never to say or do anything not entirely fitting her station. You have seen her? She often drives through the town, and then the people all run and look as pleased as if it were a holiday. We in Gerstein are quite jealous. Our duchy has no such princess to show. Do you think she is so beautiful? I have often seen her, and I do not think she is. People exaggerate everything so about a princess. My husband does not admire her at all. He says it is not what he calls classic. Her hair, for instance--but that one might get over. And people who are really beautiful always have dark eyelashes. Then her nose--my husband often laughs, and says her nose--"

"Oh," said Priscilla, faintly, "I've got a dreadful headache. I think I'll try to sleep a little if you would not mind not talking."

"Yes, that hot thing round your face must be very trying. Now if you were not so vain--what does a rash matter when only women are present? Well, well, I will not tease you. Do you know many of the Kunitzers? Do you know the Levisohns well?"

"Oh," sighed Priscilla, laying her distracted head against the cushions and shutting her eyes, "who are they?"

"Who are they? Who are the Levisohns? But dearest Fräulein if you know Kunitz you must know the Levisohns. Why, the Levisohns *are* Kunitz. They are more important far than the Grand Duke. They lend to it, and they lead it. You must know their magnificent shop at the corner of the Heiligengeiststrasse? Perhaps," she added, with a glance at the Princess's shabby serge gown, "you have not met them socially, but you must know the magnificent shop. We visit."

"Do you?" said Priscilla wearily, as the mother paused.

"And you know her story, of course?"

"Oh, oh," sighed Priscilla, turning her head from side to side on the cushions, vainly seeking peace.

"It is hardly a story for the ears of Fräuleins."

"Please don't tell it, then."

"No, I will not. It is not for Fräuleins. But one still sees she must have been a handsome woman. And he, Levisohn, was clever enough to see his way to Court favour. The Grand Duke--"

"I don't think I care to hear about the Levisohns," said Priscilla, sitting up suddenly and speaking with great distinctness. "Gossip is a thing I detest. None shall be talked in my presence."

"Hoity-toity," said the astonished mother; and it will easily be believed that no one had ever said hoity-toity to Priscilla before.

She turned scarlet under her veil. For a moment she sat with flashing eyes, and the hand lying in her lap twitched convulsively. Is it possible she was thinking of giving the comfortable mother that admonition which the policeman had so narrowly escaped? I know not what would have happened if the merry goddess, seeing things rushing to this dreadful climax, had not stopped the train in the nick of time at a wayside station and caused a breathless lady, pushing parcels before her, to clamber in. The mother's surprised stare was of necessity diverted to the new-comer. A parcel thrust into Priscilla's hands brought her back of necessity to her senses.

"*Danke, Danke*," cried the breathless lady, though no help had been offered; and hoisting herself in she wished both her fellow-passengers a boisterous good evening. The lady, evidently an able person, arranged her parcels swiftly and neatly in the racks, pulled up the windows, slammed the ventilators, stripped off her cloak, flung back her veil, and sitting down with a sigh of vast depth and length stared steadily for five minutes without wavering at the other two. At the end of that time she and the mother began, as with a common impulse, to talk. And at the end of five minutes more they had told each other where they were going, where they had been, what their husbands were, the number, age, and girth of their children, and all the adjectives that might most conveniently be used to describe their servants. The adjectives, very lurid ones, took some time. Priscilla shut her eyes while they were going on, thankful to be left quiet, feeling unstrung to the last degree; and she gradually dropped into an uneasy doze whose chief feature was the distressful repetition, like hammer-strokes on her brain, of the words, "You're deteriorating--deteriorating--deteriorating."

"*Lieber Gott,*" she whispered at last, folding her hands in her lap, "don't let me deteriorate too much. Please keep me from wanting to box people's ears. *Lieber Gott,* it's so barbarous of me. I never used to want to. Please stop me wanting to now."

And after that she dropped off quite, into a placid little slumber.

III

They crossed from Calais in the turbine. Their quickest route would have been Cologne-Ostend-Dover, and every moment being infinitely valuable Fritzing wanted to go that way, but Priscilla was determined to try whether turbines are really as steady as she had heard they were. The turbine was so steady that no one could have told it was doing anything but being quiescent on solid earth; but that was because, as Fritzing explained, there was a dead calm, and in dead calms--briefly, he explained the conduct of boats in dead calms with much patience, and Priscilla remarked when he had done that they might then, after all, have crossed by Ostend.

"We might, ma'am, and we would be in London now if we had," said Fritzing.

They had, indeed, lost several hours and some money coming by Calais, and Fritzing had lost his temper as well.

Fritzing, you remember, was sixty, and had not closed his eyes all night. He had not, so far as that goes, closed his eyes for nights without number; and what his soul had gone through during those nights was more than any soul no longer in its first youth should be called upon to bear. In the train between Cologne and Calais he had even, writhing in his seat, cursed every single one of his long-cherished ideals, called them fools, shaken his fist at them; a dreadful state of mind to get to. He did not reveal anything of this to his dear Princess, and talking to her on the turbine wore the clear brow of the philosopher; but he did feel that he was a much-tried man, and he behaved to the maid Annalise exactly in the way much-tried men do behave when they have found some one they think defenceless. Unfortunately Annalise was only apparently defenceless. Fritzing would have known it if he had been more used to running away. He did, in his calmer moments, dimly opine it. The plain fact was that Annalise held both him and Priscilla in the hollow of her hand.

At this point she had not realized it. She still was awestruck by her promotion, and looked so small and black and uncertain among her new surroundings on the turbine that if not clever of him it was at least natural that he should address her in a manner familiar to those who have had to do with men when they are being tried. He behaved, that is, to Annalise, as he had behaved to his ideals in the night; he shook his fist at her, and called her fool. It was because she had broken the Princess's umbrella. This was the new umbrella bought by him with so much trouble in Gerstein two days before, and therefore presumably of a sufficient toughness to stand any reasonable treatment for a time. There was a mist and a drizzle at Calais, and Priscilla, refusing to go under shelter, had sent Fritzing to fetch her umbrella, and when he demanded it of Annalise, she offered it him in two pieces. This alone was enough to upset a wise man, because wise men are easily upset; but Annalise declared besides that the umbrella had broken itself. It probably had. What may not one expect of anything so cheap? Fritzing, however, was maddened by this explanation, and wasted quite a long time pointing out to her in passionate language that it was an inanimate object, and that inanimate objects have no initiative and never therefore break themselves. To which Annalise, with a stoutness ominous as a revelation of character, replied by repeating her declaration that the umbrella had certainly broken itself. Then it was that he shook his fist at her and called her fool. So greatly was he moved that, after walking away and thinking it over, he went to her a second time and shook his fist at her and called her knave.

I will not linger over this of the umbrella; it teems with lessons.

While it was going on the Princess was being very happy. She was sitting unnoticed in a deck-chair and feeling she was really off at last into the Ideal. Some of us know the fascination of that feeling, and all of us know the fascination of new things; and to be unnoticed was for her of a most thrilling newness. Nobody looked at her. People walked up and down the deck in front of her as though she were not there. One hurried passenger actually tripped over her feet, and passed on with the briefest apology. Everywhere she saw indifferent faces, indifferent, oblivious faces. It was simply glorious. And she had had no trials since leaving Gerstein. There Fritzing had removed her beyond the range of the mother's eyes, grown at last extremely cold and piercing; Annalise, all meek anxiety to please, had put her to bed in the sleeping-car of the Brussels express; and in the morning her joy had been childish at having a little tray with bad coffee on it thrust in by a busy attendant, who slammed it down on the table and hurried out without so much as glancing at her. How delicious that was. The Princess laughed with delight and drank the coffee, grits and all. Oh, the blessed freedom of being insignificant. It was as good, she thought, as getting rid of your body altogether and going about an invisible spirit. She sat on the deck of the apparently motionless turbine and thought gleefully of past journeys, now for ever done with; of the grand ducal train, of herself drooping inside it as wearily as the inevitable bouquets drooping on the tables, of the crowds of starers on every platform, of the bowing officials wherever your eye chanced to turn. The Countess Disthal, of course, had been always at her elbow, and when she had to go to the window and do the gracious her anxiety lest she should bestow one smile too few had only been surpassed by the Countess's anxiety lest she should bestow one smile too many. Well, that was done with now; as much done with as a nightmare, grisly staleness, is done with when you wake to a fair spring morning and the smell of dew. And she had no fears. She was sure, knowing him as she did, that when the Grand Duke found out she had run away he would make no attempt to fetch her back, but would simply draw a line through his remembrance of her, rub her out of his mind, (his heart, she knew, would need no rubbing, because she had never been in it,) and after the first fury was over, fury solely on account of the scandal, he would be as he had been before, while she--oh wonderful new life!--she would be born again to all the charities.

Now how can I, weak vessel whose only ballast is a cargo of interrogations past which life swirls with a thunder of derisively contradictory replies, pretend to say whether Priscilla ought to have had conscience-qualms or not? Am I not deafened by the roar of answers, all seemingly so right yet all so different, that the simplest question brings? And would not the answering roar to anything so complicated as a question about conscience-qualms deafen me for ever? I shall leave the Princess, then, to run away from her home and her parent if she chooses, and make no effort to whitewash any part of her conduct that may seem black. I shall chronicle, and not comment. I shall try to, that is, for comments are very dear to me. Indeed I see I cannot move on even now till I have pointed out that though Priscilla was getting as far as she could from the Grand Duke she was also getting as near as she could to the possession of her soul; and there are many persons who believe this to be a thing so precious that it is absolutely the one thing worth living for.

The crossing to Dover, then, was accomplished quite peacefully by Priscilla. Not so, however, by Fritzing. He, tormented man, chief target for the goddess's darts, spent his time holding on to the rail along the turbine's side in order to steady himself; and as there was a dead calm that day the reader will at once perceive that the tempest must have been inside Fritzing himself. It was; and it had been raised to hurricane pitch by some snatches of the talk of two Englishmen he had heard as they paced up and down past where he was standing.

The first time they passed, one was saying to the other, "I never heard of anything so infamous."

This ought not to have made Fritzing, a person of stainless life and noble principles, start, but it did. He started; and he listened anxiously for more.

"Yes," said the other, who had a newspaper under his arm, "they deserve about as bad as they'll--"

He was out of ear-shot; but Fritzing mechanically finished the sentence himself. Who had been infamous? And what were they going to get? It was at this point that he laid hold of the handrail to steady himself till the two men should pass again.

"You can tell, of course, what steps our Government will take," was the next snatch.

"I shall be curious to see the attitude of the foreign papers," was the next.

"Anything more wanton I never heard of," was the next.

"Of all the harmless, innocent creatures--" was the next.

And the last snatch of all--for though they went on walking Fritzing heard no more after it--was the brief and singular expression "Devils."

Devils? *What* were they talking about? Devils? Was that, then, how the public stigmatized blameless persons in search of peace? Devils? What, himself and--no, never Priscilla. She was clearly the harmless innocent creature, and he must be the other thing. But why plural? He could only suppose that he and Annalise together formed a sulphurous plural. He clung very hard to the rail. Who could have dreamed it would get so quickly into the papers? Who could have dreamed the news of it would call forth such blazing words? They would be confronted at Dover by horrified authorities. His Princess was going to be put in a most impossible position. What had he done? Heavens and earth, what had he done?

He clung to the rail, staring miserably over the side into the oily water. Some of the passengers lingered to watch him, at first because they thought he was going to be seasick with so little provocation that it amounted to genius, and afterwards because they were sure he must want to commit suicide. When they found that time passed and he did neither, he became unpopular, and they went away and left him altogether and contemptuously alone.

"Fritzi, are you worried about anything?" asked Priscilla, coming to where he still stood staring, although they had got to Dover.

Worried! When all Europe was going to be about their ears? When he was in the eyes of the world a criminal--an aider, abettor, lurer-away of youth and impulsiveness? He loved the Princess so much that he cared nothing for his own risks, but what about hers? In an agony of haste he rushed to his ideals and principles for justification and comfort, tumbling them over, searching feverishly among them. They had forsaken him. They were so much lifeless rubbish. Nowhere in his mind could he find a rag of either comfort or justification with which to stop up his ears against the words of the two Englishmen and his eyes against the dreadful sight he felt sure awaited them on the quay at Dover--the sight of incensed authorities ready to pounce on him and drag him away for ever from his Princess.

Priscilla gazed at him in astonishment. He was taking no notice of her, and was looking fearfully up and down the row of faces that were watching the turbine's arrival.

"Fritzi, if you are worried it must be because you've not slept," said Priscilla, laying her hand with a stroking little movement on his sleeve; for what but overwrought nerves could make him look so odd? It was after all Fritzing who had behaved with the braveness of a lion the night before in that matter of the policeman; and it was he who had asked in stern tones of rebuke, when her courage seemed aflicker, whether she repented. "You do not repent?" she asked, imitating that sternness.

"Ma'am--" he began in a low and dreadful voice, his eyes ceaselessly ranging up and down the figures on the quay.

"Sh--sh--Niece," interrupted Priscilla, smiling.

He turned and looked at her as a man may look for the last time at the thing in life that has been most dear to him, and said nothing.

IV

But nobody was waiting for them at Dover. Fritzing's agonies might all have been spared. They passed quite unnoticed through the crowd of idlers to the train, and putting Priscilla and her maid into it he rushed at the nearest newspaper-boy, pouncing on him, tearing a handful of his papers from him, and was devouring their contents before the astonished boy had well finished his request that he should hold hard. The boy, who had been brought up in the simple faith that one should pay one's pennies first and read next, said a few things under his breath about Germans--crude short things not worth repeating--and jerking his thumb towards the intent Fritzing, winked at a detective who was standing near. The detective did not need the wink. His bland, abstracted eyes were already on Fritzing, and he was making rapid mental notes of the goggles, the muffler, the cap pulled down over the ears. Truly it is a great art, that of running away, and needs incessant practice.

And after all there was not a word about the Princess in the papers. They were full, as the Englishmen on the turbine had been full, of something the Russians, who at that time were always doing something, had just done-- something that had struck England from end to end into a blaze of indignation and that has nothing to do with my story. Fritzing dropped the papers on the platform, and had so little public spirit that he groaned aloud with relief.

"Shilling and a penny 'alfpenny, please, sir," said the newspaper-boy glibly. "*Westminster Gazette*, sir, *Daily Mail*, *Sporting and Dramatic*, one *Lady*, and two *Standards*." From which it will be seen that Fritzing had seized his handful very much at random.

He paid the boy without heeding his earnest suggestions that he should try *Tit-Bits*, the *Saturday Review*, and *Mother*, to complete, said the boy, in substance if not in words, his bird's-eye view over the field of representative English journalism, and went back to the Princess with a lighter heart than he had had for months. The detective, apparently one of Nature's gentlemen, picked up the scattered papers, and following Fritzing offered them him in the politest way imaginable just as Priscilla was saying she wanted to see what tea-baskets were like.

"Sir," said the detective, taking off his hat, "I believe these are yours."

"Sir," said Fritzing, taking off his cap in his turn and bowing with all the ceremony of foreigners, "I am much obliged to you."

"Pray don't mention it, sir," said the detective, on whose brain the three were in that instant photographed--the veiled Priscilla, the maid sitting on the edge of the seat as though hardly daring to sit at all, and Fritzing's fine head and mop of grey hair.

Priscilla, as she caught his departing eye, bowed and smiled graciously. He withdrew to a little distance, and fell into a reverie: where had he seen just that mechanically gracious bow and smile? They were very familiar to him.

As the train slowly left the station he saw the lady in the veil once more. She was alone with her maid, and was looking out of the window at nothing in particular, and the station-master, who was watching the train go, chanced to meet her glance. Again there was the same smile and bow, quite mechanical, quite absent-minded, distinctly gracious. The station-master stared in astonishment after the receding carriage. The detective roused himself from his reverie sufficiently to step forward and neatly swing himself into the guard's van: there being nothing to do in Dover he thought he would go to London.

I believe I have forgotten, in the heat of narration, to say that the fugitives were bound for Somersetshire. Fritzing had been a great walker in the days when he lived in England, and among other places had walked about Somersetshire. It is a pleasant county; fruitful, leafy, and mild. Down in the valleys myrtles and rhododendrons have been known to flower all through the winter. Devonshire junkets and Devonshire cider are made there with the same skill precisely as in Devonshire; and the parts of it that lie round Exmoor are esteemed by those who hunt.

Fritzing quite well remembered certain villages buried among the hills, miles from the nearest railway, and he also remembered the farmhouses round about these villages where he had lodged. To one of these he had caused a friend in London to write engaging rooms for himself and his niece, and there he proposed to stay till they should have found the cottage the Princess had set her heart on.

This cottage, as far as he could gather from the descriptions she gave him from time to time, was going to be rather difficult to find. He feared also that it would be a very insect-ridden place, and that their calm pursuits would often be interrupted by things like earwigs. It was to be ancient, and much thatched and latticed and rose-overgrown. It was, too, to be very small; the smallest of labourers' cottages. Yet though so small and so ancient it was to have several bathrooms--one for each of them, so he understood; "For," said the Princess, "if Annalise hasn't a bathroom how can she have a bath? And if she hasn't had a bath how can I let her touch me?"

"Perhaps," said Fritzing, bold in his ignorance of Annalise's real nature, "she could wash at the pump. People do, I believe, in the country. I remember there were always pumps."

"But do pumps make you clean enough?" inquired the Princess, doubtfully.

"We can try her with one. I fancy, ma'am, it will be less difficult to find a cottage that has only two bathrooms than one that has three. And I know there are invariably pumps."

Searching his memory he could recollect no bathrooms at all, but he did not say so, and silently hoped the best.

To the Somerset village of Symford and to the farm about a mile outside it known as Baker's, no longer, however, belonging to Baker, but rented by a Mr. Pearce, they journeyed down from Dover without a break. Nothing alarming happened on the way. They were at Victoria by five, and the Princess sat joyfully making the acquaintance of a four-wheeler's inside for twenty minutes during which Fritzing and Annalise got the luggage through the customs. Fritzing's goggles and other accessories of flight inspired so much interest in the customs that they could hardly bear to let him go and it seemed as if they would never tire of feeling about in the harmless depths of Priscilla's neat box. They had however ultimately to part from him, for never was luggage more innocent; and rattling past Buckingham Palace on the way to Paddington Priscilla blew it a cheerful kiss, symbolic of a happiness too great to bear ill-will. Later on Windsor Castle would have got one too, if it had not been so dark that she could not see it. The detective, who felt himself oddly drawn towards the trio, went down into Somersetshire by the same train as they did, but parted from them at Ullerton, the station you get out at when you go to Symford. He did not consider it necessary to go further; and taking a bedroom at Ullerton in the same little hotel from which Fritzing had ordered the conveyance that was to drive them their last seven miles he went to bed, it being close on midnight, with Mr. Pearce's address neatly written in his notebook.

This, at present, is the last of the detective. I will leave him sleeping with a smile on his face, and follow the dog-cart as it drove along that beautiful road between wooded hills that joins Ullerton to Symford, on its way to Baker's Farm.

At the risk of exhausting Priscilla Fritzing had urged pushing on without a stop, and Priscilla made no objection. This is how it came about that the ostler attached to the Ullerton Arms found himself driving to Symford in the middle of the night. He could not recollect ever having done such a thing before, and the memory of it would be quite unlikely to do anything but remain fixed in his mind till his dying day. Fritzing was a curiously conspicuous fugitive.

It was a clear and beautiful night, and the stars twinkled brightly over the black tree-tops. Down in the narrow gorge through which the road runs they could not feel the keen wind that was blowing up on Exmoor. The waters of the Sym, whose windings they followed, gurgled over their stones almost as quietly as in summer. There was a fresh wet smell, consoling and delicious after the train, the smell of country puddles and country mud and dank dead leaves that had been rained upon all day. Fritzing sat with the Princess on the back seat of the dog-cart, and busied himself keeping the rug well round her, the while his soul was full of thankfulness that their journey should after all have been so easy. He was weary in body, but very jubilant in mind. The Princess was so weary in body that she had no mind at all, and dozed and nodded and threatened to fall out, and would have fallen out a dozen times but for Fritzing's watchfulness. As for Annalise, who can guess what thoughts were hers while she was being jogged along to Baker's? That they were dark I have not a doubt. No one had told her this was to be a journey into the Ideal; no one had told her anything but that she was promoted to travelling with the Princess and that she would be well paid so long as she held her tongue. She had never travelled before, yet there were some circumstances of the journey that could not fail to strike the most inexperienced. This midnight jogging in the dog-cart, for instance. It was the second night spent out of bed, and all day long she had expected every moment would end the journey, and the end, she had naturally supposed, would be a palace. There would be a palace, and warmth, and light, and food, and welcome, and honour, and appreciative lacqueys with beautiful white silk calves--alas, Annalise's ideal, her one ideal, was to be for ever where there were beautiful white silk calves. The road between Ullerton and Symford conveyed to her mind no assurance whatever of the near neighbourhood of such things; and as for the dog-cart--"*Himmel*," said Annalise to herself, whenever she thought of the dog-cart.

Their journey ended at two in the morning. Almost exactly at that hour they stopped at the garden gate of Baker's Farm, and a woman came out with a lantern and helped them down and lighted them up the path to the porch. The Princess, who could hardly make her eyes open themselves, leaned on Fritzing's arm in a sort of confused dream, got somehow up a little staircase that seemed extraordinarily steep and curly, and was sound asleep in a knobbly bed before Annalise realized she had done with her. Priscilla had forgotten all about the Ideal, all about her eager aspirations. Sleep, dear Mother with the cool hand, had smoothed them all away, the whole rubbish of those daylight toys, and for the next twelve hours sat tenderly by her pillow, her finger on her lips.

V

No better place than Symford can be imagined for those in search of a spot, picturesque and with creepers, where they may spend quiet years guiding their feet along the way of peace. It is one of the prettiest of English villages. It does and has and is everything the ideal village ought to. It nestles, for instance, in the folds of hills; it is very small, and far away from other places; its cottages are old and thatched; its little inn is the inn of a story-book, with a quaint signboard and an apparently genial landlord; its church stands beautifully on rising ground among ancient trees, besides being hoary; its vicarage is so charming that to see it makes you long to marry a vicar; its vicar is venerable, with an eye so mild that to catch it is to receive a blessing; pleasant little children with happy morning faces pick butter-cups and go a-nutting at the proper seasons and curtsey to you as you pass; old women with clean caps and suitable faces read their Bibles behind latticed windows; hearths are scrubbed and snowy; appropriate kettles simmer on hobs; climbing roses and trim gardens are abundant; and it has a lady bountiful of so untiring a kindness that each of its female inhabitants gets a new flannel petticoat every Christmas and nothing is asked of her in return but that she shall, during the ensuing year, be warm and happy and good. The same thing was asked, I believe, of the male inhabitants, who get comforters, and also that they should drink seltzer-water whenever their lower natures urged them to drink rum; but comforters are so much smaller than petticoats that the men of Symford's sense of justice rebelled, and since the only time they ever felt really warm and happy and good was when they were drinking rum they decided that on the whole it would be more in accordance with their benefactress's wishes to go on doing it.

Lady Shuttleworth, the lady from whom these comforters and petticoats proceeded, was a just woman who required no more of others than she required of herself, and who was busy and kind, and, I am sure happy and good, on cold water. But then she did not like rum; and I suppose there are few things quite so easy as not to drink rum if you don't like it. She lived at Symford Hall, two miles away in another fold of the hills, and managed the estate of her son who was a minor--at this time on the very verge of ceasing to be one--with great precision and skill. All the old cottages in Symford were his, and so were the farms dotted about the hills. Any one, therefore, seeking a cottage would have to address himself to the Shuttleworth agent, Mr. Dawson, who too lived in a house so picturesque that merely to see it made you long either to poison or to marry Mr. Dawson--preferably, I think, to poison him.

These facts, stripped of the redundances with which I have garnished them, were told Fritzing on the day after his arrival at Baker's Farm by Mrs. Pearce the younger, old Mr. Pearce's daughter-in-law, a dreary woman with a rent in her apron, who brought in the bacon for Fritzing's solitary breakfast and the chop for his solitary luncheon. She also brought in a junket so liquid that the innocent Fritzing told her politely that he always drank his milk out of a glass when he did drink milk, but that, as he never did drink milk, she need not trouble to bring him any.

XII

It is the practice of Providence often to ignore the claims of poetic justice. Properly, the Symford children ought to have been choked by Priscilla's cakes; and if they had been, the parents who had sent them merrymaking on a Sunday would have been well punished by the undeniable awfulness of possessing choked children. But nobody was choked; and when in the early days of the following week there were in nearly every cottage pangs being assuaged, they were so naturally the consequence of the strange things that had been eaten that only Mrs. Morrison was able to see in them weapons being wielded by Providence in the cause of eternal right. She, however, saw it so plainly that each time during the next few days that a worried mother came and asked advice, she left her work or her meals without a murmur, and went to the castor-oil cupboard with an alacrity that was almost cheerful; and seldom, I suppose, have such big doses been supplied and administered as the ones she prescribed for suffering Symford.

But on this dark side of the picture I do not care to look; the party, anyhow, had been a great success, and Priscilla became at one stroke as popular among the poor of Symford as she had been in Lothen-Kunitz. Its success it is true was chiefly owing to the immense variety of things to eat she had provided; for the conjuror, merry-go-round, and cocoa-nuts to be shied at that she had told young Vickerton to bring with him from Minehead, had all been abandoned on Tussie's earnest advice, who instructed her innocent German mind that these amusements, undoubtedly admirable in themselves and on week days, were looked upon askance in England on Sundays.

"Why?" asked Priscilla, in great surprise.

"It's not keeping the day holy," said Tussie, blushing.

"How funny," said Priscilla.

"Oh, I don't know."

"Why," said Priscilla, "in Kun--" but she pulled herself up just as she was about to give him a description of the varied nature of Sunday afternoons in

Kunitz.

"You must have noticed," said Tussie, "as you have lived so long in London, that everything's shut on Sundays. There are no theatres and things--certainly no cocoa-nuts."

"No, I don't remember any cocoa-nuts," mused Priscilla, her memory going over those past Sundays she had spent in England.

Tussie tried to make amends for having obstructed her plans by exerting himself to the utmost to entertain the children as far as decorum allowed. He encouraged them to sing, he who felt every ugliness in sound like a blow; he urged them to recite for prizes of sixpences, he on whose soul Casabianca and Excelsior had much the effect of scourges on a tender skin; he led them out into a field between tea and supper and made them run races, himself setting the example, he who caught cold so easily that he knew it probably meant a week in bed. Robin helped too, but his exertions were confined to the near neighbourhood of Priscilla. His mother had been very angry with him, and he had been very angry with his mother for being angry, and he had come away from the vicarage with a bad taste in his mouth and a great defiance in his heart. It was the first time he had said hard things to her, and it had been a shocking moment,--a moment sometimes inevitable in the lives of parents and children of strong character and opposed desires. He had found himself quite unable in his anger to clothe his hard sayings in forms of speech that would have hidden their brutal force, and he had turned his back at last on her answering bitterness and fled to Baker's, thankful to find when he got there that Priscilla's beauty and the interest of the mystery that hung about her wiped out every other remembrance.

Priscilla was in the big farm kitchen, looking on at the children having tea. That was all she did at her party, except go round every now and then saying pleasant little things to each child; but this going round was done in so accomplished a manner, she seemed so used to it, was so well provided with an apparently endless supply of appropriate remarks, was so kind, and yet so--what was the word? could it be mechanical?--that Robin for the hundredth time found himself pondering over something odd, half-remembered, elusive about the girl. Then there was the uncle; manifestly a man who had never before been required to assist at a school-treat, manifestly on this occasion an unhappy man, yet look how he worked while she sat idly watching, look how he laboured round with cakes and bread-and-butter, clumsily, strenuously, with all the heat and anxiety of one eager to please and obey. Yes, that was what he did; Robin had hit on it at last. This extraordinary uncle obeyed his niece; and Robin knew very well that Germany was the last country in the world to produce men who did that. Had he not a cousin who had married a German officer? A whilom gay and sprightly cousin, who spent her time, as she dolefully wrote, having her mind weeded of its green growth of little opinions and gravelled and rolled and stamped with the opinions of her male relations-in-law. "And I'd rather have weeds than gravel," she wrote at the beginning of this process when she was still restive under the roller, "for they at least are green." But long ago she had left off complaining, long ago she too had entered into the rest that remaineth for him who has given up, who has become what men praise as reasonable and gods deplore as dull, who is tired of bothering, tired of trying, tired of everything but sleep. Then there was the girl's maid. This was the first time Robin had seen her; and while she was helping Mrs. Pearce pour out cups of chocolate and put a heaped spoonful of whipped cream on the top of each cup in the fashion familiar to Germans and altogether lovely in the eyes of the children of Symford, Robin went to her and offered help.

Annalise looked at him with heavy eyes, and shook her head.

"She don't speak no English, sir," explained Mrs. Pearce. "This one's pure heathen."

"No English," echoed Annalise drearily, who had at least learned that much, "no English, no English."

Robin gathered up his crumbs of German and presented them to her with a smile. Immediately on hearing her own tongue she flared into life, and whipping out a little pocket-book and pencil asked him eagerly where she was.

"Where you are?" repeated Robin, astonished.

"*Ja, Ja*. The address. This address. What is it? Where am I?"

"What, don't you know?"

"Tell me--quick," begged Annalise.

"But why--I don't understand. You must know you are in England?"

"England! Naturally I know it is England. But this--where is it? What is its address? For letters to reach me? Quick--tell me quick!"

Robin, however, would not be quick. "Why has no one told you?" he asked, with an immense curiosity.

"*Ach*, I have not been told. I know nothing. I am kept in the dark like--like a prisoner." And Annalise dragged her handkerchief out of her pocket, and put it to her eyes just in time to stop her ready tears from falling into the whipped cream and spoiling it.

"There she goes again," sniffed Mrs. Pearce. "It's cry, cry, from morning till night, and nothing good enough for her. It's a mercy she goes out of this to-morrow. I never see such an image."

"Tell me," implored Annalise, "tell me quick, before my mistress--"

"I'll write it for you," said Robin, taking the note-book from her. "You know you go into a cottage next week, so I'll put your new address." And he wrote it in a large round hand and gave it to her quickly, for Mrs. Pearce was listening to all this German and watching him write with a look that made him feel cheap. So cheap did it make him feel that he resisted for the present his desire to go on questioning Annalise, and putting his hands in his pockets sauntered away to the other end of the kitchen where Priscilla sat looking on. "I'm afraid that really was cheap of me," he thought ruefully, when he came once more into Priscilla's sweet presence; but he comforted himself with the reflection that no girl ought to be mysterious, and if this one chose to be so it was fair to cross her plans occasionally. Yet he went on feeling cheap; and when Tussie who was hurrying along with a cup of chocolate in each hand ran into him and spilt some on his sleeve the sudden rage with which he said "Confound you, Tussie," had little to do with the hot stuff soaking through to his skin and a great deal with the conviction that Tussie, despised from their common childhood for his weakness, smallness and ugliness, would never have done what he had just done and betrayed what the girl had chosen to keep secret from her maid.

"But why secret? Why? Why?" asked Robin, torn with desire to find out all about Priscilla.

"I'm going to do this often," said Priscilla, looking up at him with a pleased smile. "I never saw such easily amused little creatures. Don't you think it is beautiful, to give poor people a few happy moments sometimes?"

"Very beautiful," said Robin, his eyes on her face.

"It is what I mean to do in future," she said dreamily, her chin on her hand.

"It will be expensive," remarked Robin; for there were nearly two hundred children, and Priscilla had collected the strangest things in food on the long tables as a result of her method, when inviting, of asking each mother what her child best liked to eat and then ordering it with the lavishness of ignorance from Minehead.

"Oh, we shall live so simply ourselves that there will be enough left to do all I want. And it will be the most blessed change and refreshment, living simply. Fritzi hated the fuss and luxury quite as much as I did."

"Did he?" said Robin, holding his breath. The girl was evidently off her guard. He had not heard her call her uncle baldly Fritzi before; and what fuss and luxury could a German teacher's life have known?

"He it was who first made me see that the body is more than meat and the soul than raiment," mused Priscilla.

"Was he?"

"He pulled my soul out of the flesh-pots. I'm a sort of Israel come out of Egypt, but an Egypt that was altogether too comfortable."

"Too comfortable? Can one be too comfortable?"

"I was. I couldn't move or see or breathe for comfort. It was like a feather bed all over me."

"I wouldn't call that comfort," said Robin, for she paused, and he was afraid she was not going on. "It sounds much more like torture."

"So it was at last. And Fritzi helped me to shake it off. If he hadn't I'd have smothered slowly, and perhaps if I'd never known him I'd have done it as gracefully as my sisters did. Why, they don't know to this day that they are dead."

Robin was silent. He was afraid to speak lest anything he said should remind her of the part she ought to be playing. He had no doubt now at all that she was keeping a secret. A hundred questions were burning on his lips. He hated himself for wanting to ask them, for being so inquisitive, for taking advantage of the girl's being off her guard, but what are you to do with your inherited failings? Robin's mother was inquisitive and it had got into his blood, and I know of no moral magnesia that will purify these things away. "You said the other day," he burst out at last, quite unable to stop himself, "that you only had your uncle in the world. Are your sisters-- are they in London?"

"In London?" Priscilla gazed at him a moment with a vague surprise. Then fright flashed into her eyes. "Did I not tell you they were dead? Smothered?" she said, getting up quickly, her face setting into the frown that had so chilled Tussie on the heath.

"But I took that as a parable."

"How can I help how you took it?"

And she instantly left him and went away round the tables, beginning those little pleasant observations to the children again that struck him as so strange.

Well did he know the sort of thing. He had seen Lady Shuttleworth do it fifty times to the tenants, to the cottagers, at flower-shows, bazaars, on all occasions of public hospitality or ceremony; but practised and old as Lady Shuttleworth was this girl seemed yet more practised. She was a finished artist in the work, he said to himself as he leaned against the wall, his handsome face flushed, his eyes sulky, watching her. It was enough to make any good-looking young man sulky, the mixture of mystery and aloofness about Miss Neumann-Schultz. Extraordinary as it seemed, up to this point he had found it quite impossible to indulge with her in that form of more or less illustrated dialogue known to Symford youths and maidens as billing and cooing. Very fain would Robin have billed and have cooed. It was a practice he excelled in. And yet though he had devoted himself for three whole days, stood on ladders, nailed up creepers, bought and carried rum, had a horrible scene with his mother because of her, he had not got an inch nearer things personal and cosy. Miss Neumann-Schultz thanked him quite kindly and graciously for his pains--oh, she was very gracious; gracious in the sort of way Lady Shuttleworth used to be when he came home for the holidays and she patted his head and uttered benignities--and having thanked, apparently forgot him till the next time she wanted anything.

"Fritzi," said Priscilla, when in the course of her progress down the room she met that burdened man, "I'm dreadfully afraid I've said some foolish things."

Fritzing put the plate of cake he was carrying down on a dresser and wiped his forehead. "Ma'am," he said looking worried, "I cannot watch you and administer food to these barbarians simultaneously. If your tongue is so unruly I would recommend complete silence."

"I've said something about my sisters."

"Sisters, ma'am?" said Fritzing anxiously.

"Does it matter?"

"Matter? I have carefully instructed the woman Pearce, who has certainly informed, as I intended she should inform, the entire village, that you were my brother's only child. Consequently, ma'am, you have no sisters."

Priscilla made a gesture of despair. "How fearfully difficult it is not to be straightforward," she said.

"Yes, ma'am, it is. Since we started on this adventure the whole race of rogues has become the object of my sincerest admiration. What wits, what quickness, what gifts--so varied and so deftly used--what skill in deception, what resourcefulness in danger, what self-command--"

"Yes but Fritzi what are we to do?"

"Do, ma'am? About your royal sisters? Would to heaven I had been born a rogue!"

"Yes, but as you were not--ought I to go back and say they're only half-sisters? Or step-sisters? Or sisters in law? Wouldn't that do?"

"With whom were you speaking?"

"Mr. Morrison."

"Ma'am, let me beg you to be more prudent with that youth than with any one. Our young friend Cæsar Augustus is I believe harmlessness itself compared with him. Be on your guard, ma'am. Curb that fatal feminine appendage, your tongue. I have remarked that he watches us. But a short time since I saw him eagerly conversing with your Grand Ducal Highness's maid. For me he has already laid several traps that I have only just escaped falling into by an extraordinary presence of mind and a nimbleness in dialectic almost worthy of a born rogue."

"Oh Fritzi," said the frightened Priscilla, laying her hand on his sleeve, "do go and tell him I didn't mean what I said."

Fritzing wiped his brow again. "I fail to understand," he said, looking at Priscilla with worried eyes, "what there is about us that can possibly attract any one's attention."

"Why, there isn't anything," said Priscilla, with conviction. "We've been most careful and clever. But just now--I don't know why--I began to think aloud."

"Think aloud?" exclaimed Fritzing, horrified. "Oh ma'am let me beseech you never again to do that. Better a thousand times not to think at all. What was it that your Grand Ducal Highness thought aloud?"

And Priscilla, shamefaced, told him as well as she could remember.

"I will endeavour to remedy it," said poor Fritzing, running an agitated hand through his hair.

Priscilla sighed, and stood drooping and penitent by the dresser while he went down the room to where Robin still leaned against the wall.

"Sir," said Fritzing--he never called Robin young man, as he did Tussie-- "my niece tells me you are unable to distinguish truth from parable."

"What?" said Robin staring.

"You are not, sir, to suppose that when my niece described her sisters as dead that they are not really so."

"All right sir," said Robin, his eyes beginning to twinkle.

"The only portion of the story in which my niece used allegory was when she described them as having been smothered. These young ladies, sir, died in the ordinary way, in their beds."

"Feather beds, sir?" asked Robin briskly.

"Sir, I have not inquired into the nature of the beds," said Fritzing with severity.

"Is it not rather unusual," asked Robin, "for two young ladies in one family to die at once? Were they unhealthy young ladies?"

"Sir, they did not die at once, nor were they unhealthy. They were perfectly healthy until they--until they began to die."

"Indeed," said Robin, with an interest properly tinged with regret. "At least, sir," he added politely, after a pause in which he and Fritzing stared very hard at each other, "I trust I may be permitted to express my sympathy."

"Sir, you may." And bowing stiffly Fritzing returned to Priscilla, and with a sigh of relief informed her that he had made things right again.

"Dear Fritzi," said Priscilla looking at him with love and admiration, "how clever you are."

XIII

It was on the Tuesday, the day Priscilla and Fritzing left Baker's and moved into Creeper Cottage, that the fickle goddess who had let them nestle for more than a week beneath her wing got tired of them and shook them out. Perhaps she was vexed by their clumsiness at pretending, perhaps she thought she had done more than enough for them, perhaps she was an epicure in words and did not like a cottage called Creeper; anyhow she shook them out. And if they had had eyes to see they would not have walked into their new home with such sighs of satisfaction and such a comfortable feeling that now at last the era of systematic serenity and self-realization, beautifully combined with the daily exercise of charity, had begun; for waiting for them in Priscilla's parlour, established indeed in her easy-chair by the fire and warming her miserable toes on the very hob, sat grey Ill Luck horribly squinting.

Creeper Cottage, it will be remembered, consisted of two cottages, each with two rooms, an attic, and a kitchen, and in the back yard the further accommodation of a coal-hole, a pig-stye, and a pump. Thanks to Tussie's efforts more furniture had been got from Minehead. Tussie had gone in himself, after a skilful questioning of Fritzing had made him realize how little had been ordered, and had, with Fritzing's permission, put the whole thing into the hands of a Minehead firm. Thus there was a bed for Annalise and sheets for everybody, and the place was as decent as it could be made in the time. It was so tiny that it got done, after a great deal of urging from Tussie, by the Tuesday at midday, and Tussie himself had superintended the storing of wood in the coal-hole and the lighting of the fire that was to warm his divine lady and that Ill Luck found so comforting to her toes. The Shuttleworth horses had a busy time on the Friday, Saturday, and Monday, trotting up and down between Symford and Minehead; and the Shuttleworth servants and tenants, not being more blind than other people, saw very well that their Augustus had lost his heart to the lady from nowhere. As for Lady Shuttleworth, she only smiled a rueful smile and stroked her poor Tussie's hair in silence when, having murmured something about the horses being tired, he reproved her by telling her that it was everybody's duty to do what they could for strangers in difficulties.

Priscilla's side of Creeper Cottage was the end abutting on the churchyard, and her parlour had one latticed window looking south down the village street, and one looking west opening directly on to the churchyard. The long grass of the churchyard, its dandelions and daisies, grew right up beneath this window to her wall, and a tall tombstone half-blocked her view of the elm-trees and the church. Over this room, with the same romantic and gloomy outlook, was her bedroom. Behind her parlour was what had been the shoemaker's kitchen, but it had been turned into a temporary bathroom. True no water was laid on as yet, but the pump was just outside, and nobody thought there would be any difficulty about filling the bath every morning by means of the pump combined with buckets. Over the bathroom was the attic. This was Annalise's bedroom. Nobody thought there would be any difficulty about that either; nobody, in fact, thought anything about anything. It was a simple place, after the manner of attics, with a window in its sloping ceiling through which stars might be studied with great comfort as one lay in bed. A frugal mind, an earnest soul, would have liked the attic, would have found a healthy enjoyment in a place so plain and fresh, so swept in windy weather by the airs of heaven. A poet, too, would certainly have flooded any parts of it that seemed dark with the splendour of his own inner light; a nature-lover, again, would have quickly discovered the spiders that dwelt in its corners, and spent profitable hours on all fours observing them. But an Annalise--what was she to make of such a place? Is it not true that the less a person has inside him of culture and imagination the more he wants outside him of the upholstery of life? I think it is true; and if it is, then the vacancy of Annalise's mind may be measured by the fact that what she demanded of life in return for the negative services of not crying and wringing her hands was nothing less filled with food and sofas and servants than a grand ducal palace.

But neither Priscilla nor Fritzing knew anything of Annalise's mind, and if they had they would instantly have forgotten it again, of such extreme unimportance would it have seemed. Nor would I dwell on it myself if it were not that its very vacancy and smallness was the cause of huge upheavals in Creeper Cottage, and the stone that the builders ignored if they did not actually reject behaved as such stones sometimes do and came down upon the builders' heads and crushed them. Annalise, you see, was unable to appreciate peace, yet on the other hand she was very able to destroy the peace of other people; and Priscilla meant her cottage to be so peaceful--a temple, a holy place, within whose quiet walls sacred years were going to be spent in doing justly, in loving mercy, in walking humbly. True she had not as yet made a nearer acquaintance with its inconveniences, but anyhow she held the theory that inconveniences were things to be laughed at and somehow circumvented, and that they do not enter into the consideration of persons whose thoughts are absorbed by the burning desire to live out their ideals. "You can be happy in any place whatever," she remarked to Tussie on the Monday, when he was expressing fears as to her future comfort; "absolutely any place will do--a tub, a dingle, the top of a pillar--any place at all, if only your soul is on fire."

"Of course you can," cried Tussie, ready to kiss her feet.

"And look how comfortable my cottage seems," said Priscilla, "directly one compares it with things like tubs."

"Yes, yes," agreed Tussie, "I do see that it's enough for free spirits to live in. I was only wondering whether--whether bodies would find it enough."

"Oh bother bodies," said Priscilla airily.

But Tussie could not bring himself to bother bodies if they included her own; on the contrary, the infatuated young man thought it would be difficult sufficiently to cherish a thing so supremely precious and sweet. And each time he went home after having been in the frugal baldness of Creeper Cottage he hated the superfluities of his own house more and more, he accused himself louder and louder of being mean-spirited, effeminate, soft, vulgar, he loathed himself for living embedded in such luxury while she, the dear and lovely one, was ready cheerfully to pack her beauty into a tub if needs be, or let it be weather-beaten on a pillar for thirty years if by so doing she could save her soul alive. Tussie at this time became unable to see a sleek servant dart to help him take off his coat without saying something sharp to him, could not sit through a meal without making bitter comparisons between what they were eating and what the poor were probably eating, could not walk up his spacious staircase and along his lofty corridors without scowling; they, indeed, roused his contemptuous wrath in quite a special degree, the reason being that Priscilla's stairs, the stairs up and down which her little feet would have to clamber daily, were like a ladder, and she possessed no passages at all. But what of that? Priscilla could not see that it mattered, when Tussie drew her attention to it.

Both Fritzing's and her front door opened straight into their sitting-rooms; both their staircases walked straight from the kitchens up into the rooms above. They had meant to have a door knocked in the dividing wall downstairs, but had been so anxious to get away from Baker's that there was no time. In order therefore to get to Fritzing Priscilla would have either to go out into the street and in again at his front door, or go out at her back door and in again at his. Any meals, too, she might choose to have served alone would have to be carried round to her from the kitchen in Fritzing's half, either through the backyard or through the street.

Tussie thought of this each time he sat at his own meals, surrounded by deft menials, lapped as he told himself in luxury,--oh, thought Tussie writhing, it was base. His much-tried mother had to listen to many a cross and cryptic remark flung across the table from the dear boy who had always been so gentle; and more than that, he put his foot down once and for all and refused with a flatness that silenced her to eat any more patent foods. "Absurd," cried Tussie. "No wonder I'm such an idiot. Who could be anything else with his stomach full of starch? Why, I believe the stuff has filled my veins with milk instead of good honest blood."

"Dearest, I'll have it thrown out of the nearest window," said Lady Shuttleworth, smiling bravely in her poor Tussie's small cross face. "But what shall I give you instead? You know you won't eat meat."

"Give me lentils," cried Tussie. "They're cheap."

"Cheap?"

"Mother, I do think it offensive to spend much on what goes into or onto one's body. Why not have fewer things, and give the rest to the poor?"

"But I do give the rest to the poor; I'm always doing it. And there's quite enough for us and for the poor too."

"Give them more, then. Why," fumed Tussie, "can't we live decently? Hasn't it struck you that we're very vulgar?"

"No, dearest, I can't say that it has."

"Well, we are. Everything we have that is beyond bare necessaries makes us vulgar. And surely, mother, you do see that that's not a nice thing to be."

"It's a horrid thing to be," said his mother, arranging his tie with an immense and lingering tenderness.

"It's a difficult thing not to be," said Tussie, "if one is rich. Hasn't it struck you that this ridiculous big house, and the masses of things in it, and the whole place and all the money will inevitably end by crushing us both out of heaven?"

"No, I can't say it has. I expect you've been thinking of things like the eyes of needles and camels having to go through them," said his mother, still patting and stroking his tie.

"Well, that's terrifically true," mused Tussie, reflecting ruefully on the size and weight of the money-bags that were dragging him down into darkness. Then he added suddenly, "Will you have a small bed--a little iron one--put in my bedroom?"

"A small bed? But there's a bed there already, dear."

"That big thing's only fit for a sick woman. I won't wallow in it any longer."

"But dearest, all your forefathers wallowed, as you call it, in it. Doesn't it seem rather--a pity not to carry on traditions?"

"Well mother be kind and dear, and let me depart in peace from them. A camp bed,--that's what I'd like. Shall I order it, or will you? And did I tell you I've given Bryce the sack?"

"Bryce? Why, what has he done?"

"Oh he hasn't done anything that I know of, except make a sort of doll or baby of me. Why should I be put into my clothes and taken out of them again as though I hadn't been weaned yet?"

Now all this was very bad, but the greatest blow for Lady Shuttleworth fell when Tussie declared that he would not come of age. The cheerful face with which his mother had managed to listen to his other defiances went very blank at that; do what she would she could not prevent its falling. "Not come of age?" she repeated stupidly. "But my darling, you can't help yourself--you must come of age."

"Oh I know I can't help being twenty-one and coming into all this"--and he waved contemptuous arms--"but I won't do it blatantly."

"I--I don't understand," faltered Lady Shuttleworth.

"There mustn't be any fuss, mother."

"Do you mean no one is to come?"

"No one at all, except the tenants and people. Of course they are to have their fun--I'll see that they have a jolly good time. But I won't have our own set and the relations."

"Tussie, they've all accepted."

"Send round circulars."

"Tussie, you are putting me in a most painful position."

"Dear mother, I'm very sorry for that. I wish I'd thought like this sooner. But really the idea is so revolting to me--it's so sickening to think of all these people coming to pretend to rejoice over a worm like myself."

"Tussle, you are not a worm."

"And then the expense and waste of entertaining them--the dreariness, the boredom--oh, I wish I only possessed a tub--one single tub--or had the pluck to live like Lavengro in a dingle."

"It's quite impossible to stop it now," interrupted Lady Shuttleworth in the greatest distress; of Lavengro she had never heard.

"Yes you can, mother. Write and put it off."

"Write? What could I write? To-day is Tuesday, and they all arrive on Friday. What excuse can I make at the last moment? And how can a birthday be put off? My dearest boy, I simply can't." And Lady Shuttleworth, the sensible, the cheery, the resourceful, the perennially brave, wrung her hands and began quite helplessly to cry.

This unusual and pitiful sight at once conquered Tussie. For a moment he stood aghast; then his arms were round his mother, and he promised everything she wanted. What he said to her besides and what she sobbed back to him I shall not tell. They never spoke of it again; but for years they both looked back to it, that precious moment of clinging together with bursting hearts, her old cheek against his young one, her tears on his face, as to one of the most acutely sweet, acutely, painfully, tender experiences of their joint lives.

It will be conceded that Priscilla had achieved a good deal in the one week that had passed since she laid aside her high estate and stepped down among ordinary people for the purpose of being and doing good. She had brought violent discord into a hitherto peaceful vicarage, thwarted the hopes of a mother, been the cause of a bitter quarrel between her and her son, brought out by her mysteriousness a prying tendency in the son that might have gone on sleeping for ever, entirely upset the amiable Tussie's life by rending him asunder with a love as strong as it was necessarily hopeless, made his mother anxious and unhappy, and, what was perhaps the greatest achievement of all, actually succeeded in making that mother cry. For of course Priscilla was the ultimate cause of these unusual tears, as Lady Shuttleworth very well knew. Lady Shuttleworth was the deceased Sir Augustus's second wife, had married him when she was over forty and well out of the crying stage, which in the busy does not last beyond childhood, had lost him soon after Tussie's birth, had cried copiously and most properly at his funeral, and had not cried since. It was then undoubtedly a great achievement on the part of the young lady from nowhere, this wringing of tears out of eyes that had been dry for one and twenty years. But the list of what Priscilla had done does not end with this havoc among mothers. Had she not interrupted the decent course of Mrs. Jones's dying, and snatched her back to a hankering after the unfit? Had she not taught the entire village to break the Sabbath? Had she not made all its children either sick or cross under the pretence of giving them a treat? On the Monday she did something else that was equally well-meaning, and yet, as I shall presently relate, of disastrous consequences: she went round the village from cottage to cottage making friends with the children's mothers and leaving behind her, wherever she went, little presents of money. She had found money so extraordinarily efficacious in the comforting of Mrs. Jones that before she started she told Fritzing to fill her purse well, and in each cottage it was made somehow so clear how badly different things were wanted that the purse was empty before she was half round the village and she had to go back for a fresh supply. She was extremely happy that afternoon, and so were the visited mothers. They, indeed, talked of nothing else for the rest of the day, discussed it over their garden hedges, looked in on each other to compare notes, hurried to meet their husbands on their return from work to tell them about it, and were made at one stroke into something very like a colony of eager beggars. And in spite of Priscilla's injunction to Mrs. Jones to hide her five-pound note all Symford knew of that as well, and also of the five-pound note Mrs. Morrison had taken away. Nothing was talked of in Symford but Priscilla. She had in one week created quite a number of disturbances of a nature fruitful for evil in that orderly village; and when on the Tuesday she and Fritzing moved into Creeper Cottage they were objects of the intensest interest to the entire country side, and the report of their riches, their recklessness, and their eccentric choice of a dwelling had rolled over the intervening hills as far as Minehead, where it was the subject of many interesting comments in the local papers.

They got into their cottage about tea time; and the first thing Priscilla did was to exclaim at the pleasant sight of the wood fire and sit down in the easy-chair to warm herself. We know who was sitting in it already; and thus she was received by Bad Luck at once into her very lap, and clutched about securely by that unpleasant lady's cold and skinny arms. She looked up at Fritzing with a shiver to remark wonderingly that the room, in spite of its big fire and its smallness, was like ice, but her lips fell apart in a frozen stare and she gazed blankly past him at the wall behind his head. "Look," she whispered, pointing with a horrified forefinger. And Fritzing, turning quickly, was just in time to snatch a row of cheap coloured portraits from the wall and fling them face downwards under the table before Tussie came in to ask if he could do anything.

The portraits were those of all the reigning princes of Germany and had been put up as a delicate compliment by the representative of the Minehead furnishers, while Priscilla and Fritzing were taking leave of Baker's Farm; and the print Priscilla's eye had lighted on was the portrait of her august parent, smiling at her. He was splendid in state robes and orders, and there was a charger, and an obviously expensive looped-up curtain, and much smoke as of nations furiously raging together in the background, and outside this magnificence meandered the unmeaning rosebuds of Priscilla's cheap wallpaper. His smile seemed very terrible under the circumstances. Fritzing felt this, and seized him and flung him with a desperate energy under the table, where he went on smiling, as Priscilla remembered with a guilty shudder, at nothing but oilcloth. "I don't believe I'll sleep if I know he--he's got nothing he'd like better than oilcloth to look at," she whispered with an awestruck face to Fritzing as Tussie came in.

"I will cause them all to be returned," Fritzing assured her.

"What, have those people sent wrong things?" asked Tussie anxiously, who felt that the entire responsibility of this *ménage* was on his shoulders.

"Oh, only some cheap prints," said Priscilla hastily. "I think they're called oleographs or something."

"What impertinence," said Tussie hotly.

"I expect it was kindly meant, but I--I like my cottage quite plain."

"I'll have them sent back, sir," Tussie said to Fritzing, who was rubbing his hands nervously through his hair; for the sight of his grand ducal master's face smiling at him on whom he would surely never wish to smile again, and doing it, too, from the walls of Creeper Cottage, had given him a shock.

"You are ever helpful, young man," he said, bowing abstractedly and going away to put down his hat and umbrella; and Priscilla, with a cold feeling that she had had a bad omen, rang the handbell Tussie's thoughtfulness had placed on her table and ordered Annalise to bring tea.

Now Annalise had been standing on the threshold of her attic staring at it in an amazement too deep for words when the bell fetched her down. She appeared, however, before her mistress with a composed face, received the order with her customary respectfulness, and sought out Fritzing to inquire of him where the servants were to be found. "Her Grand Ducal Highness desires tea," announced Annalise, appearing in Fritzing's sitting-room, where he was standing absorbed in the bill from the furnishers that he had found lying on his table.

"Then take it in," said Fritzing impatiently, without looking up.

"To whom shall I give the order?" inquired Annalise.

"To whom shall you give the order?" repeated Fritzing, pausing in his study to stare at her, the bill in one hand and his pocket-handkerchief, with which he was mopping his forehead, in the other.

"Where," asked Annalise, "shall I find the cook?"

"Where shall you find the cook?" repeated Fritzing, staring still harder. "This house is so gigantic is it not," he said with an enormous sarcasm, "that no doubt the cook has lost himself. Have you perhaps omitted to investigate the coal-hole?"

"Herr Geheimrath, where shall I find the cook?" asked Annalise tossing her head.

"Fräulein, is there a mirror in your bedroom?"

"The smallest I ever saw. Only one-half of my face can I see reflected in it at a time."

"Fräulein, the half of that face you see reflected in it is the half of the face of the cook."

"I do not understand," said Annalise.

"Yet it is as clear as shining after rain. You, *mein liebes Kind*, are the cook."

It was now Annalise's turn to stare, and she stood for a moment doing it, her face changing from white to red while Fritzing turned his back and taking out a pencil made little sums on the margin of the bill. "Herr Geheimrath, I am not a cook," she said at last, swallowing her indignation.

"What, still there?" he exclaimed, looking up sharply. "Unworthy one, get thee quickly to the kitchen. Is it seemly to keep the Princess waiting?"

"I am not a cook," said Annalise defiantly. "I was not engaged as a cook, I never was a cook, and I will not be a cook."

Fritzing flung down the bill and came and glared close into Annalise's face. "Not a cook?" he cried. "You, a German girl, the daughter of poor parents, you are not ashamed to say it? You do not hide your head for shame? No--a being so useful, so necessary, so worthy of respect as a cook you are not and never will be. I'll tell you what you are,--I've told you once already, and I repeat it--you are a knave, my Fräulein, a knave, I say. And in those parts of your miserable nature where you are not a knave--for I willingly concede that no man or woman is bad all through--in those parts, I say, where your knavishness is intermittent, you are an absolute, unmitigated fool."

"I will not bear this," cried Annalise.

"Will not! Cannot! Shall not! Inept Negation, get thee to thy kitchen and seek wisdom among the pots."

"I am no one's slave," cried Annalise, "I am no one's prisoner."

"Hark at her! Who said you were? Have I not told you the only two things you are?"

"But I am treated as a prisoner, I am treated as a slave," sobbed Annalise.

"Unmannerly one, how dare you linger talking follies when your royal mistress is waiting for her tea? Run--run! Or must I show you how?"

"Her Grand Ducal Highness," said Annalise, not budging, "told me also to prepare the bath for her this evening."

"Well, what of that?" cried Fritzing, snatching up the bill again and adding up furiously. "Prepare it, then."

"I see no water-taps."

"Woman, there are none."

"How can I prepare a bath without water-taps?"

"O thou Inefficiency! Ineptitude garbed as woman! Must I then teach thee the elements of thy business? Hast thou not observed the pump? Go to it, and draw water. Cause the water to flow into buckets. Carry these buckets--need I go on? Will not Nature herself teach thee what to do with buckets?"

Annalise flushed scarlet. "I will not go to the pump," she said.

"What, you will not carry out her Grand Ducal Highness's orders?"

"I will not go to the pump."

"You refuse to prepare the bath?"

"I will not go to the pump."

"You refuse to prepare the tea?"

"I will not be a cook."

"You are rankly rebellious?"

"I will not sleep in the attic."

"What!"

"I will not eat the food."

"What!"

"I will not do the work."

"What!"

"I will go."

"Go?"

"*Go*," repeated Annalise, stamping her foot. "I demand my wages, the increased wages that were promised me, and I will go."

"And where, Impudence past believing, will you go, in a country whose tongue you most luckily do not understand?"

Annalise looked up into Fritzing's furious eyes with the challenge of him who flings down his trump card. "Go?" she cried, with a defiance that was blood-curdling in one so small and hitherto so silent, "I will first go to that young gentleman who speaks my language and I will tell him all, and then, with his assistance, I will go straight--but *straight*, do you hear?"--and she stamped her foot again--"to Lothen-Kunitz."

XIV

Early in this story I pointed out what to the intelligent must have been from the beginning apparent, that Annalise held Priscilla and Fritzing in the hollow of her hand. In the first excitement of the start she had not noticed it, but during those woeful days of disillusionment at Baker's she saw it with an ever-growing clearness; and since Sunday, since the day she found a smiling young gentleman ready to talk German to her and answer questions, she was perfectly aware that she had only to close her hand and her victims would squeeze into any shape she liked. She proposed to do this closing at the first moment of sheer intolerableness, and that moment seemed well reached when she entered Creeper Cottage and realized what the attic, the kitchen, and the pump really meant.

It is always a shock to find one's self in the company of a worm that turns, always a shock and an amazement; a spectacle one never, somehow, gets used to. But how dreadful does it become when one is in the power of the worm, and the worm is resentful, and ready to squeeze to any extent. Fritzing reflected bitterly that Annalise might quite well have been left at home. Quite well? A thousand times better. What had she done but whine during her passive period? And now that she was active, a volcano in full activity hurling forth hot streams of treachery on two most harmless heads, she, the insignificant, the base-born, the empty-brained, was actually going to be able to ruin the plans of the noblest woman on earth.

Thus thought Fritzing, mopping his forehead. Annalise had rushed away to her attic after flinging her defiance at him, her spirit ready to dare anything but her body too small, she felt, to risk staying within reach of a man who looked more like somebody who meant to shake her than any one she had ever seen. Fritzing mopped his forehead, and mopped and mopped again. He stood where she had left him, his eyes fixed on the ground, his distress so extreme that he was quite near crying. What was he to do? What was he to say to his Princess? How was he to stop the girl's going back to Kunitz? How was he to stop her going even so far as young Morrison? That she should tell young Morrison who Priscilla was would indeed be a terrible thing. It would end their being able to live in Symford. It would end their being able to live in England. The Grand Duke would be after them, and there would have to be another flight to another country, another start there, another search for a home, another set of explanations, pretences, fears, lies,--things of which he was so weary. But there was something else, something worse than any of these things, that made Fritzing mop his forehead with so extreme a desperation: Annalise had demanded the money due to her, and Fritzing had no money.

I am afraid Fritzing was never meant for a conspirator. Nature never meant him to be a plotter, an arranger of unpleasant surprises for parents. She never meant him to run away. She meant him, probably, to spend his days communing with the past in a lofty room with distempered walls and busts round them. That he should be forced to act, to decide, to be artful, to wrangle with maids, to make ends meet, to squeeze his long frame and explosive disposition into a Creeper Cottage where only an ill-fitting door separated him from the noise and fumes of the kitchen, was surely a cruel trick of Fate, and not less cruel because he had brought it on himself. That he should have thought he could run away as well as any man is merely a proof of his singleness of soul. A man who does that successfully is always, among a great many other things, a man who takes plenty of money with him and knows exactly where to put his hand on more when it is wanted. Fritzing had thought it better to get away quickly with little money than to wait and get away with more. He had seized all he could of his own that was not invested, and Priscilla had drawn her loose cash from the Kunitz bank; but what he took hidden in his gaiters after paying for Priscilla's outfit and bribing Annalise was not more than three hundred pounds; and what is three hundred pounds to a person who buys and furnishes cottages and scatters five-pound notes among the poor? The cottages were paid for. He had insisted on doing that at once, chiefly in order to close his dealings with Mr. Dawson; but Mr. Dawson had not let them go for less than a hundred and fifty for the two, in spite of Tussie's having said a hundred was enough. When Fritzing told Mr. Dawson what Tussie had said Mr. Dawson soon proved that Tussie could not possibly have meant it; and Fritzing, knowing how rich Priscilla really was and what vast savings he had himself lying over in Germany in comfortable securities, paid him without arguing and hastened from the hated presence. Then the journey for the three from Kunitz had been expensive; the stay at Baker's Farm had been, strange to say, expensive; Mrs. Jones's comforting had been expensive; the village mothers had twice emptied Priscilla's purse of ten pounds; and the treat to the Symford children had not been cheap. After paying for this--the

Minehead confectioner turned out to be a man of little faith in unknown foreigners, and insisted on being paid at once--Fritzing had about forty pounds left. This, he had thought, would do for food and lights and things for a long while,--certainly till he had hit on a plan by which he would be able to get hold of the Princess's money and his own without betraying where they were; and here on his table, the second unpleasant surprise that greeted him on entering his new home (the first had been his late master's dreadful smile) was the bill for the furnishing of it. To a man possessed of only forty pounds any bill will seem tremendous. This one was for nearly two hundred; and at the end of the long list of items, the biggest of which was that bathroom without water that had sent Annalise out on strike, was the information that a remittance would oblige. A remittance! Poor Fritzing. He crushed the paper in his hand and made caustic mental comments on the indecency of these people, clamouring for their money almost before the last workman was out of the place, certainly before the smell of paint was out of it, and clamouring, too, in the face of the Shuttleworth countenance and support. He had not been a week yet in Symford, and had been so busy, so rushed, that he had put off thinking out a plan for getting his money over from Germany until he should be settled. Never had he imagined people would demand payment in this manner. Never, either, had he imagined the Princess would want so much money for the poor; and never, of course, had he imagined that there would be a children's treat within three days of their arrival. Least of all had he dreamed that Annalise would so soon need more bribing; for that was clearly the only thing to do. He saw it was the only thing, after he had stood for some time thinking and wiping the cold sweat from his forehead. She must be bribed, silenced, given in to. He must part with as much as he possibly could of that last forty pounds; as much, also, as he possibly could of his pride, and submit to have the hussy's foot on his neck. Some day, some day, thought Fritzing grinding his teeth, he would be even with her; and when that day came he promised himself that it should certainly begin with a sound shaking. "Truly," he reflected, "the foolish things of the world confound the wise, and the weak things of the world confound the things that are mighty." And he went out, and standing in the back yard beneath Annalise's window softly called to her. "Fräulein," called Fritzing, softly as a dove wooing its mate.

"Aha," thought Annalise, sitting on her bed, quick to mark the change; but she did not move.

"Fräulein," called Fritzing again; and it was hardly a call so much as a melodious murmur.

Annalise did not move, but she grinned.

"Fräulein, come down one moment," cooed Fritzing, whose head was quite near the attic window so low was Creeper Cottage. "I wish to speak to you. I wish to give you something."

Annalise did not move, but she stuffed her handkerchief into her mouth; for the first time since she left Calais she was enjoying herself.

"If," went on Fritzing after an anxious pause, "I was sharp with you just now--and I fear I may have been hasty--you should not take it amiss from one who, like Brutus, is sick of many griefs. Come down, Fräulein, and let me make amends."

The Princess's bell rang. At once habit impelled Annalise to that which Fritzing's pleadings would never have effected; she scrambled down the ladder, and leaving him still under her window presented herself before her mistress with her usual face of meek respect.

"I said tea," said Priscilla very distinctly, looking at her with slightly lifted eyebrows.

Annalise curtseyed and disappeared.

"How fearfully polite German maids are," remarked Tussie.

"In what way?" asked Priscilla.

"Those curtseys. They're magnificent."

"Don't English maids curtsey?"

"None that I've ever seen. Perhaps they do to royalties."

"Oh?" said Priscilla with a little jump. She was still so much unnerved by the unexpected meeting with her father on the wall of Creeper Cottage that she could not prevent the little jump.

"What would German maids do, I wonder, in dealing with royalties," said Tussie, "if they curtsey so beautifully to ordinary mistresses? They'd have to go down on their knees to a princess, wouldn't they?"

"How should I know?" said Priscilla, irritably, alarmed to feel she was turning red; and with great determination she began to talk literature.

Fritzing was lying in wait for Annalise, and caught her as she came into the bathroom.

"Fräulein," said the miserable man trying to screw his face into persuasiveness, "you cannot let the Princess go without tea."

"Yes I can," said Annalise.

He thrust his hands into his pockets to keep them off her shoulders.

"Make it this once, Fräulein, and I will hire a woman of the village to make it in future. And see, you must not leave the Princess's service, a service of such great honour to yourself, because I chanced to be perhaps a little-- hasty. I will give you two hundred marks to console you for the slight though undoubted difference in the mode of living, and I will, as I said, hire a woman to come each day and cook. Will it not be well so?"

"No," said Annalise.

"No?"

Annalise put her hands on her hips, and swaying lightly from side to side began to sing softly. Fritzing gazed at this fresh development in her manners in silent astonishment. "*Jedermann macht mir die Cour, c'est l'amour, c'est l'amour,*" sang Annalise, her head one side, her eyes on the ceiling.

"*Liebes Kind,* are your promises of no value? Did you not promise to keep your mouth shut, and not betray the Princess's confidence? Did she not seek you out from all the others for the honour of keeping her secrets? And you will, after one week, divulge them to a stranger? You will leave her service? You will return to Kunitz? Is it well so?"

"*C'est l'amour, c'est l'amour,*" sang Annalise, swaying.

"Is it well so, Fräulein?" repeated Fritzing, strangling a furious desire to slap her.

"Did you speak?" inquired Annalise, pausing in her song.

"I am speaking all the time. I asked if it were well to betray the secrets of your royal mistress."

"I have been starved," said Annalise.

"You have had the same fare as ourselves."

"I have been called names."

"Have I not expressed--regret?"

"I have been treated as dirt."

"Well, well, I have apologized."

"If you had behaved to me as a maid of a royal lady should be behaved to, I would have faithfully done my part and kept silence. Now give me my money and I will go."

"I will give you your money--certainly, *liebes Kind.* It is what I am most desirous of doing. But only on condition that you stay. If you go, you go without it. If you stay, I will do as I said about the cook and will--" Fritzing paused--"I will endeavour to refrain from calling you anything hasty."

"Two hundred marks," said Annalise gazing at the ceiling, "is nothing."

"Nothing?" cried Fritzing. "You know very well that it is, for you, a great sum."

"It is nothing. I require a thousand."

"A thousand? What, fifty English sovereigns? Nay, then, but there is no reasoning with you," cried Fritzing in tones of real despair.

She caught the conviction in them and hesitated. "Eight hundred, then," she said.

"Impossible. And besides it would be a sin. I will give you twenty."

"Twenty? Twenty marks?" Annalise stared at him a moment then resumed her swaying and her song--"*Jedermann macht mir die Cour*"--sang Annalise with redoubled conviction.

"No, no, not marks--twenty pounds," said Fritzing, interrupting what was to him a most maddening music. "Four hundred marks. As much as many a German girl can only earn by labouring two years you will receive for doing nothing but hold your tongue."

Annalise closed her lips tightly and shook her head. "My tongue cannot be held for that," she said, beginning to sway again and hum.

Adjectives foamed on Fritzing's own, but he kept them back. "*Mädchen*," he said with the gentleness of a pastor in a confirmation class, "do you not remember that the love of money is the root of all evil? I do not recognize you. Since when have you become thus greedy for it?"

"Give me eight hundred and I will stop."

"I will give you six hundred," said Fritzing, fighting for each of his last precious pounds.

"Eight."

"Six."

"I said eight," said Annalise, stopping and looking at him with lifted eyebrows and exactly imitating the distinctness with which the Princess had just said "I said tea."

"Six is an enormous sum. Why, what would you do with it?"

"That is my affair. Perhaps buy food," she said with a malicious sideglance.

"I tell you there shall be a cook."

"A cook," said Annalise counting on her fingers,--"and a good cook, observe--not a cook like the Frau Pearce--a cook, then, no more rude names, and eight hundred marks. Then I stop. I suffer. I am silent."

"It cannot be done. I cannot give you eight."

"*C'est l'amour, c'est l'amour....* The Princess waits for her tea. I will prepare it for her this once. I am good, you see, at heart. But I must have eight hundred marks. *Cest l'amo-o-o-o-our.*"

"I will give you seven," said Fritzing, doing rapid sums in his head. Seven hundred was something under thirty-five pounds. He would still have five pounds left for housekeeping. How long that would last he admitted to himself that probably only heaven knew, but he hoped that with economy it might be made to carry them over a fortnight; and surely by the end of a fortnight he would have hit on a way of getting fresh supplies from Germany? "I will give you seven hundred. That is the utter-most. I can give no more till I have written home for money. I have only a little more than that here altogether. See, I treat you like a reasonable being--I set the truth plainly before you. More than seven hundred I could not give if I would."

"Good," said Annalise, breaking off her music suddenly. "I will take that now and guarantee to be silent for fourteen days. At the end of that time the Herr Geheimrath will have plenty more money and will, if he still desires my services and my silence, give me the three hundred still due to me on the thousand I demand. If the Herr Geheimrath prefers not to, then I depart to my native country. While the fortnight lasts I will suffer all there is to suffer in silence. Is the Herr Geheimrath agreed?"

"Shameless one!" mentally shrieked Fritzing, "Wait and see what will happen to thee when my turn comes!" But aloud he only agreed. "It is well, Fräulein," he said. "Take in the Princess's tea, and then come to my sitting-room and I will give you the money. The fire burns in the kitchen. Utensils, I believe, are ready to hand. It should not prove a task too difficult."

"Perhaps the Herr Geheimrath will show me where the tea and milk is? And also the sugar, and the bread and butter if any?" suggested Annalise in a small meek voice as she tripped before him into the kitchen.

What could he do but follow? Her foot was well on his neck; and it occurred to him as he rummaged miserably among canisters that if the creature should take it into her head to marry him he might conceivably have to let her do it. As it was it was he and not Annalise who took the kettle out to the pump to fill it, and her face while he was doing it would have rejoiced her parents or other persons to whom she was presumably dear, it was wide with so enormous a satisfaction. Thus terrible is it to be in the power of an Annalise.

XV

The first evening in Creeper Cottage was unpleasant. There was a blazing wood fire, the curtains were drawn, the lamp shone rosily through its red shade, and when Priscilla stood up her hair dusted the oak beams of the ceiling, it was so low. The background, you see, was perfectly satisfactory; exactly what a cottage background should be on an autumn night when outside a wet mist is hanging like a grey curtain across the window panes; and Tussie arriving at nine o'clock to help consecrate the new life with Shakespeare felt, as he opened the door and walked out of the darkness into the rosy, cosy little room, that he need not after all worry himself with doubts as to the divine girl's being comfortable. Never did place appear more comfortable. It did not occur to him that a lamp with a red shade and the blaze of a wood fire will make any place appear comfortable so long as they go on shining, and he looked up at Priscilla--I am afraid he had to look up at her when they were both standing--with the broadest smile of genuine pleasure. "It *does* look jolly," he said heartily.

His pleasure was doomed to an immediate wiping out. Priscilla smiled, but with a reservation behind her smile that his sensitive spirit felt at once. She was alone, and there was no sign whatever either of her uncle or of preparations for the reading of Shakespeare.

"Is anything not quite right?" Tussie asked, his face falling at once to an anxious pucker.

Priscilla looked at him and smiled again, but this time the smile was real, in her eyes as well as on her lips, dancing in them together with the flickering firelight. "It's rather funny," she said. "It has never happened to me before. What do you think? I'm hungry."

"Hungry?"

"Hungry."

Tussie stared, arrested in the unwinding of his comforter.

"Really hungry. *Dreadfully* hungry. So hungry that I hate Shakespeare."

"But--"

"I know. You're going to say why not eat? It does seem simple. But you've no idea how difficult it really is. I'm afraid my uncle and I have rather heaps to learn. We forgot to get a cook."

"A cook? But I thought--I understood that curtseying maid of yours was going to do all that?"

"So did I. So did he. But she won't."

Priscilla flushed, for since Tussie left after tea she had had grievous surprises, of a kind that made her first indignant and then inclined to wince. Fritzing had not been able to hide from her that Annalise had rebelled and refused to cook, and Priscilla had not been able to follow her immediate impulse and dismiss her. It was at this point, when she realized this, that the wincing began. She felt perfectly sick at the thought, flashed upon her for the first time, that she was in the power of a servant.

"Do you mean to say," said Tussie in a voice hollow with consternation, "that you've had no dinner?"

"Dinner? In a cottage? Why of course there was no dinner. There never will be any dinner--at night, at least. But the tragic thing is there was no supper. We didn't think of it till we began to get hungry. Annalise began first. She got hungry at six o'clock, and said something to Fritz--my uncle about it, but he wasn't hungry himself then and so he snubbed her. Now he is hungry himself, and he's gone out to see if he can't find a cook. It's very stupid. There's nothing in the house. Annalise ate the bread and things she found. She's upstairs now, crying." And Priscilla's lips twitched as she looked at Tussie's concerned face, and she began to laugh.

He seized his hat. "I'll go and get you something," he said, dashing at the door.

"I can't think what, at this time of the night. The only shop shuts at seven."

"I'll make them open it."

"They go to bed at nine."

"I'll get them out of bed if I have to shie stones at their windows all night."

"Don't go without your coat--you'll catch a most frightful cold."

He put his arm through the door to take it, and vanished in the fog. He did not put on the coat in his agitation, but kept it over his arm. His comforter stayed in Priscilla's parlour, on the chair where he had flung it. He was in evening dress, and his throat was sore already with the cold that was coming on and that he had caught, as he expected, running races on the Sunday at Priscilla's children's party.

Priscilla went back to her seat by the fire, and thought very hard about things like bread. It would of course be impossible that she should have reached this state of famine only because one meal had been missed; but she had eaten nothing all day,--disliked the Baker's Farm breakfast too much even to look at it, forgotten the Baker's Farm dinner because she was just moving into her cottage, and at tea had been too greatly upset by the unexpected appearance of her father on the wall to care to eat the bread and butter Annalise brought in. Now she was in that state when you tremble and feel cold. She had told Annalise, about half-past seven, to bring her the bread left from tea, but Annalise had eaten it. At half-past eight she had told Annalise to bring her the sugar, for she had read somewhere that if you eat enough sugar it takes away the desire even of the hungriest for other food, but Annalise, who had eaten the sugar as well, said that the Herr Geheimrath must have eaten it. It certainly was not there, and neither was the Herr Geheimrath to defend himself; since half-past seven he had been out looking for a cook, his mind pervaded by the idea that if only he could get a cook food would follow in her wake as naturally as flowers follow after rain. Priscilla fretting in her chair that he should stay away so long saw very clearly that no cook could help them. What is the use of a cook in a house where there is nothing to cook? If only Fritzing would come back quickly with a great many loaves of bread! The door was opened a little way and somebody's knuckles knocked. She thought it was Tussie, quick and clever as ever, and in a voice full of welcome told him to come in; upon which in stepped Robin Morrison very briskly, delighted by the warmth of the invitation. "Why now this *is* nice," said Robin, all smiles.

Priscilla did not move and did not offer to shake hands, so he stood on the hearthrug and spread out his own to the blaze, looking down at her with bright, audacious eyes. He thought he had not yet seen her so beautiful. There was an extraordinary depth and mystery in her look, he thought, as it rested for a moment on his face, and she had never yet dropped her eyelashes as she now did when her eyes met his. We know she was very hungry, and there was no strength in her at all. Not only did her eyelashes drop, but her head as well, and her hands hung helplessly, like drooping white flowers, one over each arm of the chair.

"I came in to ask Mr. Neumann-Schultz if there's anything I can do for you," said Robin.

"Did you? He lives next door."

"I know. I knocked there first, but he didn't answer so I thought he must be here."

Priscilla said nothing. At any other time she would have snubbed Robin and got rid of him. Now she merely sat and drooped.

"Has he gone out?"

"Yes."

Her voice was very low, hardly more than a whisper. Those who know the faintness of hunger at this stage will also know the pathos that steals into the voice of the sufferer when he is unwillingly made to speak; it becomes plaintive, melodious with yearning, the yearning for food. But if you do not know this, if you have yourself just come from dinner, if you are half in love and want the other person to be quite in love, if you are full of faith in your own fascinations, you are apt to fall into Robin's error and mistake the nature of the yearning. Tussie in Robin's place would have doubted the evidence of his senses, but then Tussie was very modest. Robin doubted nothing. He saw, he heard, and he thrilled; and underneath his thrilling, which was real enough to make him flush to the roots of his hair, far down underneath it was the swift contemptuous comment, "They're all alike."

Priscilla shut her eyes. She was listening for the first sound of Tussie's or Fritzing's footfall, the glad sound heralding the approach of something to eat, and wishing Robin would go away. He was kind at times and obliging, but on the whole a nuisance. It was a great pity there were so many people in the world who were nuisances and did not know it. Somebody ought to tell them,--their mothers, or other useful persons of that sort. She vaguely decided that the next time she met Robin and was strengthened properly by food she would say a few things to him from which recovery would take a long while.

"Are you--not well?" Robin asked, after a silence during which his eyes never left her and hers were shut; and even to himself his voice sounded deeper, more intense than usual.

"Oh yes," murmured Priscilla with a little sigh.

"Are you--happy?"

Happy? Can anybody who is supperless, dinnerless, breakfastless, be happy, Priscilla wondered? But the question struck her as funny, and the vibrating tones in which it was asked struck her as rather funny too, and she opened her eyes for a moment to look up at Robin with a smile of amusement--a smile that she could not guess was turned by the hunger within her into something wistful and tremulous. "Yes," said Priscilla in that strange pathetic voice, "I--think so." And after a brief glance at him down went her weary eyelids again.

The next thing that happened was that Robin, who was trembling, kissed her hand. This she let him do with perfect placidity. Every German woman is used to having her hand kissed. It is kissed on meeting, it is kissed on parting, it is kissed at a great many odd times in between; she holds it up mechanically when she comes across a male acquaintance; she is never surprised at the ceremony; the only thing that surprises her is if it is left out. Priscilla then simply thought Robin was going. "What a mercy," she said to herself, glancing at him a moment through her eyelashes. But Robin was not used to hand-kissing and saw things in a very different light. He felt she made no attempt to draw her hand away, he heard her murmuring something inarticulate--it was merely Good-bye--he was hurled along to his doom; and stooping over her the unfortunate young man kissed her hair.

Priscilla opened her eyes suddenly and very wide. I don't know what folly he would have perpetrated next, or what sillinesses were on the tip of his tongue, or what meaning he still chose to read in her look, but an instant afterwards he was brought down for ever from the giddy heights of his illusions: Priscilla boxed his ears.

I am sorry to have to record it. It is always sweeter if a woman does not box ears. The action is shrewish, benighted, mediæval, nay, barbarous; and this box was a very hard one indeed, extraordinarily hard for so little a hand and so fasting a girl. But we know she had twice already been on the verge of doing it; and the pent-up vigour of what the policeman had not got and what the mother in the train had not got was added I imagine to what Robin got. Anyhow it was efficacious. There was an exclamation--I think of surprise, for surely a young man would not have minded the pain?--and he put his hand up quickly to his face. Priscilla got up just as quickly out of her chair and rang the handbell furiously, her eyes on his, her face ablaze. Annalise must have thrown herself down the ladder, for they hardly seemed to have been standing there an instant face to face, their eyes on a level, he scarlet, she white, both deadly silent, before the maid was in the room.

"This person has insulted me," said Priscilla, turning to her and pointing at Robin. "He never comes here again. Don't let me find you forgetting that," she added, frowning at the girl; for she remembered they had been seen talking eagerly together at the children's treat.

"I never"--began Robin.

"Will you go?"

Annalise opened the door for him. He went out, and she shut it behind him. Then she walked sedately across the room again, looking sideways at the Princess, who took no notice of her but stood motionless by the table gazing straight before her, her lips compressed, her face set in a kind of frozen white rage, and having got into the bathroom Annalise began to run. She ran out at the back door, in again at Fritzing's back door, out at his front door into the street, and caught up Robin as he was turning down the lane to the vicarage. "What have you done?" she asked him breathlessly, in German.

"Done?" Robin threw back his head and laughed quite loud.

"Sh--sh," said Annalise, glancing back fearfully over her shoulder.

"Done?" said Robin, subduing his bitter mirth. "What do you suppose I've done? I've done what any man would have in my place--encouraged, almost asked to do it. I kissed your young lady, *liebes Fräulein,* and she pretended not to like it. Now isn't that what a sensible girl like you would call absurd?"

But Annalise started back from the hand he held out to her in genuine horror. "What?" she cried, "What?"

"What? What?" mocked Robin. "Well then, what? Are you all such prudes in Germany? Even you pretending, you little hypocrite?"

"Oh," cried Annalise hysterically, pushing him away with both her hands, "what have you done? *Elender Junge*, what have you done?"

"I think you must all be mad," said Robin angrily. "You can't persuade me that nobody ever kisses anybody over in Germany."

"Oh yes they do--oh yes they do," cried Annalise, wringing her hands, "but neither there nor anywhere else--in England, anywhere in the world--do the sons of pastors--the sons of pastors--" She seemed to struggle for breath, and twisted and untwisted her apron round her hands in a storm of agitation while Robin, utterly astonished, stared at her--"Neither there nor anywhere else do they--the sons of pastors--kiss--kiss royal princesses."

It was now Robin's turn to say "What?"

XVI

He went up to Cambridge the next morning. Term had not begun, but he went; a Robin with all the briskness gone out of him, and if still with something of the bird left only of a bird that is moulting. His father was mildly surprised, but applauded the apparent desire for solitary study. His mother was violently surprised, and tried hard to get at his true reasons. She saw with the piercing eye of a relation--that eye from which hardly anything can ever be hidden--that something had happened and that the something was sobering and unpleasant. She could not imagine what it was,